SKUNK

and

BADGER

ALSO BY AMY TIMBERLAKE

One Came Home
a Newbery Honor book
an Edgar Award winner

That Girl Lucy Moon

The Dirty Cowboy
illustrated by Adam Rex

SKUNK

and

BADGER

by Amy Timberlake

with pictures by Jon Klassen

HARPERCOLLINS PUBLISHERS LTD

For Phil

Published by HarperCollins Publishers Ltd by arrangement
with Algonquin Young Readers, an imprint of Algonquin Books of Chapel Hill,
a division of Workman Publishing Co., Inc.

First Canadian edition

HarperCollins Publishers Ltd
Bay Adelaide Centre, East Tower
22 Adelaide Street West, 41st Floor
Toronto, Ontario, Canada
M5H 4E3

www.harpercollins.ca

Library and Archives Canada Cataloguing in Publication

Title: Skunk and badger / by Amy Timberlake ; with pictures by Jon Klassen.
Names: Timberlake, Amy, author. | Klassen, Jon, illustrator.
Identifiers: Canadiana (print) 20200272020 | Canadiana (ebook) 2020027208X |
ISBN 9781443460453 (hardcover) | ISBN 9781443460460 (ebook)
Classification: LCC PZ7.T515 Sku 2020 | DDC j813/.6—dc23

Design by Carla Weise

Printed and bound in the United States of America
LSC/H 9 8 7 6 5 4 3 2 1

CHAPTER ONE

THE FIRST TIME BADGER SAW SKUNK, HE THOUGHT, *PUNY*, and shut the front door.

Badger didn't normally shut the door on animals that knocked. But there was too much slick in this one's stripe, too much puff in his tail. Also, there'd been that grin, and the way he'd stuck out his paw as if he had been looking forward to meeting Badger for a long, long time.

Badger knew what to make of that. He shut the door before the fellow got any ideas. "Not. Buying. Anything," he said through the keyhole.

When the knocking continued, Badger added, "Ever."

Then he drew the bolt.

And the double bolt.

And latched the chain.

Quartzite! Badger thought briskly as he padded back into his rock room.

Aunt Lula's brownstone row house had not come with a rock room. Badger had made improvements. He had dragged out the sofa and cushy chairs. He'd boxed the books and board games. He'd closed up the fireplace. Then he'd pushed in his rock table and his stool and aligned his work light. Over the fireplace, he had hung his rock hammers and saws. His rock tumbler fit on the window seat. The bookshelves had been a good place for boxes of rocks and minerals. He'd shelved them alphabetically with the most delicate specimens wrapped in tissue paper. In the fireplace, Badger had piled geodes in a pyramid. (*Artistic!*) Finally, Badger had shoved open the pocket doors, clearing a path into the kitchen for a paw-full of dry cereal, and declared his rock room complete.

Now Badger pulled his stool up to his rock table. He adjusted his work light. He picked up a magnifying glass with one paw and the quartzite with the other.

Rap-rap. Rap-rap-rap.

The sound came from the front door. Badger stopped. It was that fellow again.

Badger put down the magnifying glass and the quartzite, and opened his calendar. No appointments. No fix-it animals. The Yard Sheep grazed the lawn on Saturday. In fact, today's calendar square contained an *X*. *X* meant "IMPORTANT ROCK WORK."

Of course, this being Aunt Lula's brownstone, Aunt Lula could stop by anytime. But she would not knock. Aunt Lula had a key.

Badger remembered how Aunt Lula had helped him out: Three years ago, he had been a rock scientist without steady rock work or a good den to live in. The situation worsened until one day, Aunt Lula offered her brownstone as a place for Badger to live.

"Untilyougetbackonyourfeet," said Aunt Lula, who was a pine marten and said everything quickly.

Aunt Lula offered the brownstone for free. "Youarefamily! Mynephew!"

Scientific funding! A long-term residency! A grant of time and space! Badger had thought.

Anyway, Aunt Lula almost never visited. She wrote letters. An image of the mail pail sitting on the desk in his bedroom flashed into Badger's mind. It contained two, if not three, unopened letters from Aunt Lula.

Must read those, Badger thought.

Rap-rap-rap. Rap.

Badger frowned. Surely the fellow wouldn't keep on knocking?

Rap. Rap. Rap.

Badger decided he would ignore the rapping. The fellow would be forced to go away. He rotated the quartzite, held the magnifying glass over a promising crystal, and leaned.

"Badger?" came a voice through the keyhole.

Badger froze.

"Badger? Are you in there?" came the voice again.

Badger dropped the quartzite. The quartzite shattered.

"Sludge and slurry!"

"Badger?" *Rap-rap-rap.*

Badger stared at the shards of quartzite. He looked in the direction of the front door. Then he set down his magnifying glass, stood up, and walked to the rock tumbler. He flipped the switch to On. The water in the tumbler sloshed. The grit in the tumbler ground. The rocks *chip-chip-chip*ped and the motor whined as the tumbler turned *ErrrrrRRRRR* over . . . and *ErrrrrRRRRR* over . . . and *ErrrrrRRRRR* over again.

Badger sighed. His shoulders settled. He swept up his shattered quartzite and selected another rock. He sat down at

4

his rock table, picked up the magnifying glass, and held it over the rock.

Concentrate, he told himself when he sensed movement in the windows behind him.

Badger concentrated for one (*one thousand*), two (*one thousand*), three (*one thousand*) seconds and then thought, *How does he know my name?* The nameplate on the letter box read, LULA P. MARTEN.

A thought followed: *What if he is Someone Important?*

Badger raced through the front hallway, threw back the bolts, unlatched the chain, and opened the door.

No one was there.

"Hello? Anybody?" called Badger.

A bird sang. A breeze twisted past. The air smelled of honey.

He stepped out onto the stoop. The letter box and flowerpot were empty. He did not find anything tacked to the back of the door. Badger frowned. *Someone Important would have left a note.*

On the sidewalk below, a gray-and-white-speckled chicken stopped. It eyed Badger—first with the left eye, then with the right.

A chicken? In North Twist? Badger never saw chickens.

"Bock bock," the chicken said. It stood with its neck upstretched, eyeing him right-left, left-right.

Badger had the oddest feeling he was supposed to say something. *To a chicken?*

"Bock?" said the chicken.

"Shoo! Shoo!" When the chicken didn't move, Badger waved his paws. "Go on now—shoo!"

"Bock!" The chicken fluttered off, past a small red suitcase tied shut with twine. The suitcase sat at the bottom of Badger's stoop.

Badger moaned. *Quick—inside!*

But that was when the fellow came around the corner, picked up the suitcase, and dashed up the steps. Before Badger knew it, his paw was being given a vigorous shake.

"Badger, I am Skunk! I have heard much about you. It is so good to finally meet!" Skunk's grin was so large, and his paw-shaking so energetic, that Badger's insides warmed.

"Oh," said Badger, blushing.

And in that moment, Skunk squeezed past Badger and entered the brownstone.

Like that! thought Badger.

As Badger shut the door, he knew there'd be no stopping Skunk's game plan. The red suitcase would be popped open to reveal something guaranteed to change everything. Next would come the patter, the pitch, the easy payment plan. "A real game changer!" he'd be told. The talking would go on and on.

He found Skunk in his rock room. (*My rock room!*) Skunk peered. He poked the pile of geodes in the fireplace.

6

"Great place. Nice kitchen." Skunk nodded appreciatively. He twirled one of Badger's rock hammers in his right paw.

Badger took the hammer. "Rock hammers are not toys."

Skunk shook his head. "Definitely not! It would be good for mashing potatoes, though."

Badger put the hammer away with emphasis, and noticed the red suitcase tied up with twine. The suitcase sat in the center of the room. Badger looked at it suggestively.

Skunk followed Badger's gaze to the red suitcase, looked back at Badger, and gave him a wide smile. "I am here!"

"You are," said Badger.

There was a pause.

Followed by another pause.

Skunk pointed at the rock tumbler. "I switched it to Off. That machine is loud. It sounds like it is shaking rocks. Ha!"

"It is a rock *tumbler*," said Badger. "It *polishes* rocks."

"Oh," said Skunk. "May I see a polished rock?"

"No."

"Oh." Skunk blinked, sighed, and sat down.

On my rock stool! thought Badger. Badger stared at Skunk sitting on his rock stool.

Skunk stared back at him, and then set his chin in a paw, and began to twist ever so slightly, back and forth, on the rock stool.

"Ahem," said Badger.

Skunk glanced up.

Badger looked pointedly at the suitcase.

Skunk also looked at the suitcase, frowned at Badger, and said, "This is a good stool. It spins. You must like spinning. I also like to spin. Watch!" Skunk gripped the sides of the stool and kicked off.

"You must stop now!" said Badger.

Skunk stopped with a skid.

And said nothing!

Badger began to pace. "Look, there are not ten steps that will improve my life. I already manage my time. I do not spend money on raffles or lottery tickets. I have no holes in my socks. I do not believe in X-ray glasses or fungus powders. Fake diamond rings fail to impress. I do not need a blender, and I certainly do not need a shoehorn. Unless you are here with money to fund a rock scientist doing Important Rock Work—which, I might add, I do relentlessly, tirelessly, and with more grit than a wad of gum—there is nothing you can offer me. Not interested. No thank you." Badger stopped in front of Skunk. "So may we get on with our lives now?" He moved in the direction of the door.

Skunk sat up. "Horns for your shoes? Shoehorns sound necessary."

Badger laughed. "Har! That's true! Good one! Shoehorns!"

Then Badger realized he'd been diverted. He crossed his arms. "No more funny business. Do you have rocks in that suitcase? If you have rocks, I'm interested."

Skunk gave him a look. "Why would I have rocks in my suitcase? Everyone knows rocks are heavy." Skunk took in the room. "You do like rocks. There are *a lot* of rocks in this room."

Badger gasped in exasperation. "So what's in the suitcase?"

Skunk blinked. "My storybook. A chicken whistle. Pajamas." Then he grinned. "I get it! Is there a secret code word? Aunt Lula forgot to tell me the secret code word."

Badger swayed on his feet. "Aunt Lula?"

"Yes, Aunt Lula said you would give me a room and a key." Skunk hopped off the rock stool. "I am your new roommate, Skunk!" Then Skunk tilted his head. "Did you think I was a door-to-door sales skunk? That is funny. Ha!"

"Har-har!" Badger laughed politely, while inwardly everything lurched. *A roommate? No! Not possible!* Aunt Lula would have told him.

Badger remembered—again—the two (maybe three?) unread letters from Aunt Lula sitting in his mail pail.

But then a piece of information, something he'd read, came to mind. He *chuck-chuck*ed at Skunk and shook his head. "Aunt

9

Lula? *Aunt?* You're a skunk. I am a badger. We are not family. That's scientifically proven!"

Skunk laughed. "I know! But Aunt Lula insisted I call her 'Aunt.' I thought it best to agree. Have you ever won an argument with Aunt Lula? Pine martens speak so fast." Skunk added with a shrug, "Aunt Lula did know my mother."

Badger blurted, "Don't you have your own home?"

Skunk flinched and took a step back.

"Well?" Badger heard himself say.

Skunk looked at Badger and rubbed a paw through his stripe. "I did have a home," he said.

Badger raised an eyebrow.

Skunk looked away, fiddled with his tail, and then deflated. He met Badger's eyes and whispered, "Not everyone wants a skunk."

As soon as he finished whispering those words, Skunk jerked upright. With a hop, he snatched his red suitcase off the floor. "I am sorry. This is so-so, so-so, *so* embarrassing. Aunt Lula said she had written and told you. Maybe she forgot? I would not like to think she forgot, but maybe she did? Pine martens do everything fast. Sometimes I wonder how they remember to do what they said they would do, especially when they say things so speedily. Aunt Lula said it like this: Skunkyoumust goandlivewithBadgerinmybrownstoneinNorthTwist. Youwill likehim. Youwillbegoodgoodgoodgoodgoodfriends. Iwill writehimimmediately!"

Badger had to admit that this sounded like Aunt Lula.

Also: He had not read those letters.

Also: The brownstone belonged to Aunt Lula.

Therefore: There was nothing to be done.

Skunk, though, was making for the door. "I will find somewhere else to stay. You did not know I was coming."

Badger raced in front of Skunk and said what needed to be said: "Oh, you're *that* Skunk! Come in, come in! It is good to finally meet you!"

CHAPTER TWO

"CONSIDER YOURSELF MY SPECIAL GUEST!" BADGER plucked the red suitcase from Skunk's grasp with one paw, and took firm hold of Skunk's elbow with the other. He steered Skunk away from the front door.

"Here! We! Are!" Badger stopped at the end of the hallway. With a dramatic sweep, he gestured at a folding door. He set down the suitcase, pulled open the door, and tugged a chain.

The bulb flickered on.

"Ta-da! My Special Guest Closet! There's even a place for belongings." Badger patted the shelf above.

Skunk squinted into the closet, taking in the luggage-rack bed with T-shirt bedding and balled-athletic-sock pillow.

The bulb hummed fluorescently.

"Oh," said Skunk finally. He paused and pointed toward the stairs. "Aren't there rooms up there? On the second floor? Aunt Lula told me—"

"Never!" Badger interrupted. He leapt into the center of the hallway. "I couldn't—no *wouldn't*—do that to you. You are my Special Guest. You *deserve* to stay in my Special Guest Closet."

Skunk leaned to see up the stairs. He looked up at Badger. He glanced into the closet and then at his suitcase. Finally, he shrugged. "Okay."

"Good," said Badger.

Skunk brushed off his paws. "That is settled. Now please tell me where the neighborhood chickens congregate. I would like to make their acquaintance." Skunk paused and then added, "I will need that key to the brownstone. Chickens have no sense of time. I have known some very late chickens. I would not want to wake you by coming in late."

"Chickens? There aren't chickens in this neighborhood." As he said this, Badger remembered the chicken he had seen from the stoop.

"Ha!" laughed Skunk. "You are funny! Even I know there are lots of chickens in this neighborhood. I have seen three Orpingtons and one leghorn and I just got here."

Skunk picked up his red suitcase and plunked it on top of the luggage-rack bed.

The bed toppled. The light went out.

"Unpack! Get comfortable! I'll find the spare key!" Badger called over his shoulder as he sprinted up the stairs.

———◄○►———

It did not take Badger long to find the spare key. He pawed the key over to Skunk then raced back upstairs to his bedroom. *Mail pail! Now!*

In his mail pail, Badger found four letters (*four letters!*) from Aunt Lula.

The first letter was all this, that, and the other thing. Badger tossed it into the trash bin. The second letter blithered and blathered its way through most of a page, and then the word appeared: "Skunk." Badger gulped, backed up, and read the sentence he'd skated by. Aunt Lula had met Skunk. She had been "such good friends" with Skunk's mother.

Badger tore into the third envelope, shook out the paper, and read, read, read. The entire third letter–all five slogging pages of it–prattled on about Skunk and Skunk's mother. It ended: "What would you think of Skunk moving into the brownstone? I am sure you will like him! Please respond as soon as possible."

A muttering began: "Did not respond. *Certainly* did not respond. What have I done?"

Badger was so distressed he tore the fourth letter in half. After taping the two halves back together, he read:

Dear Badger,

I am sending Skunk to the brownstone. Please welcome him! He is a delight!

As I did for you, I've given Skunk permission to stay in my brownstone for as long as he'd like. Give him a big room on the second floor and keys to come and go. He'll be a wonderful roommate!

I hope this arrangement doesn't come as a shock. In a previous letter I asked for your thoughts but have heard nothing. I would wait for a reply, but Skunk's living situation is precarious, so I will take your lack of response as agreement. I expect you're busy with Important Rock Work!

It makes me smile to think of you and Skunk together. I look forward to news of your adventures!

Hugs,

Aunt Lula

Roommate? Room on the second floor? Stay as long as he likes? Badger groaned and flopped belly-first onto his bed.

He flipped over, stared at the ceiling, and thought, *As she did for me?* He clenched and unclenched the bedding in his paw. He turned his head to take in his rock scientist diploma and his three blue ribbons hanging on the wall. Badger had been a rock scientist in need of funding. He did Important Rock Work!

What did this Skunk bring to the brownstone? A *chicken whistle?* Whatever that was, Badger wasn't falling for it.

Also, Badger's suitcase latched on its own. It did not require twine.

"Not everyone wants a skunk," Skunk had said.

Got that right.

———◆———

Badger spent that evening in his bedroom. When bedtime came, he tossed and turned and stared vaguely at the ceiling.

There is only one thing to do, he thought finally. Badger rolled off the bed, crawled to the closet, pulled out the case, and unlatched it. "Ukulele," he whispered, as he tucked its koa-wood body under his elbow. He took a deep breath and plucked.

Pliiinggg, sounded the ukulele.

Badger sighed.

He plucked another string: *Pliiinggg.* He sighed again.

He ran a claw over all four strings: *Beed . . . el . . . lee . . . bing!*

The sound rang out. Hastily, Badger clapped a paw over the ukulele's sound hole. "Shhh!" he whispered.

Still, he plucked the bottom string one more time: *Pliiiinggg.*

Gently, Badger set the ukulele back in its case, latched the latches (*c-click, c-click*), and slid the case into the back of his closet.

The *pliiiinggg* stayed with him as he climbed into bed. Wrapped in the ring of the note, Badger slept.

———◁o▷———

The next morning Badger awoke to smells. *Eggs . . . onions and . . .*

"Cinnamon," Badger mumbled.

A dream, thought Badger. In his kitchen one thing—and one thing only—awaited him: cold cereal in a cold bowl with cold milk. Again.

He turned over in his bed, took a deep breath, and smelled . . . *definitely cinnamon.*

Then he remembered: *That fellow! That Skunk!* Badger's eyes popped open.

He smelled something else. *Burning?*

He sniffed again. *Burning!* Coughing, Badger leapt from his bed. "Fire! Fire!" Badger yelled, as he raced down the stairs.

Skunk ran out of the kitchen. He held a pepper clamped in tongs over his head. "Fire? Where?" Skunk skittered right and looked. Skunk skidded left. The pepper at the end of Skunk's tongs trailed a long, thin line of smoke.

Skunk followed Badger's gaze. "Ha!" He jabbed the air with his pepper. "This? This is not fire. This is fire-*roasted*. It is breakfast!"

"Breakfast?" said Badger, as Skunk and the pepper disappeared back into the kitchen.

Badger stood stunned at the bottom of the stairs. *Breakfast for me too?* He listened to the sounds coming from the kitchen: The vent hood whooshed on. ("Should have turned that on sooner," he heard Skunk say.) Pans and pots clanked. Something hit something else and sizzled. Something was shaken. The faucet turned on and off. Skunk whistled a tune.

The air around Badger was thick with smells: savory and sweet, buttery, toasty and grilled. If he were a civet, he'd have wanted to roll in the smells while yelling, "Rejoice! Rejoice!" But being a badger, he tip-clawed to the kitchen for a wary peek.

From the doorway, Badger stared. The kitchen looked cozy, welcoming even. Candlelight flickered on the kitchen table. Two places were set with placemats, cloth napkins in napkin rings, a fork and a knife. Nothing matched. One napkin was purple and dotted, the other a tartan plaid, and the half-finished candle had been stuck into a bulbous bottle covered with wax drippings. But Badger found it delightful.

Skunk whirred to the stove, the counter, back to the stove, the sink, the kitchen table, and returned to the stove. He spotted Badger in the doorway. "Come in, come in. Come on in!" Skunk jabbed a spatula in the direction of a chair. "Sit. Breakfast soon." Then Skunk scraped furiously at something in a fry pan.

Badger sat.

The scraping stopped, and Skunk marched over to Badger. He put his paws on his hips and said, "I am not a baby cow. You are not a baby cow. I will not insult your palate with baby cow food. Have you ever met a baby cow? Slugs are better conversationalists. But never fear, you will like your breakfast hot chocolate fine without baby cow milk."

"Breakfast hot chocolate?" Badger did not think he would have trouble drinking breakfast hot chocolate. He was about to say this, but Skunk was already across the room at the kitchen counter. He tossed something in a bowl with a big spoon. Skunk picked up the bowl, gave it a shake, and a small potato shot across the room.

"Rocket potato! Watch out!" yelled Skunk.

"Har-HAR!" Badger laughed. "Ha!" laughed Skunk. Their eyes met, and they grinned at one another.

Then Skunk nodded seriously. "I will get Rocket Potato later." The bowl clunked back onto the counter and Skunk continued to cook.

A few minutes later, Skunk laid a plate of scrambled eggs with fire-roasted peppers in front of Badger.

Badger knew what to do next. He forked it up and put it in his mouth. "Oh . . . mmmm."

Skunk shook out a napkin. "Tuck this under your chin."

Badger tucked the napkin under his chin and forked up more eggs. "Mmmm . . . mahMah."

Thereafter followed the promised breakfast hot chocolate— *yes!*—and a basket of strawberry cinnamon muffins. (*A basket!*) After everything else came roasted fingerling potatoes. Skunk apologized for the potatoes coming last: "I get the eating order wrong sometimes, but with breakfast I do not mind terribly." Skunk sat down with his own plate of potatoes. "Breakfast is the nicest meal," he said.

Badger nodded vigorously.

Skunk continued: "Because breakfast is the nicest meal, you should have candlelight at breakfast. If at all possible. Sometimes it is not possible. Sometimes you are eating where there is not a candle. Or sometimes there is a candle shortage, and no one has candles. That is sad, particularly for breakfast."

Breakfast is the nicest meal.

"Yes . . . Mahmmm," said Badger, hiding his mouthful with a paw.

Skunk clapped his paws. "I knew it. We are so much alike. We will be good roommates."

Then—with Skunk at one end of the table and Badger at the other—they turned to their plates and ate.

Badger was into his fourth muffin (*fifth muffin? Sixth?*) when he realized that things had gone silent.

Also, the candle had snuffed out.

Badger looked up from his plate. Skunk was not at his spot at the kitchen table.

He surveyed the room. Skunk was not in front of the stove. Bowls, plates, a cutting board, and cooking doodads and gizmos littered the counters. Something oozed off a fry pan onto a burner.

No one was cleaning up.

Then an image of a small potato streaking across the kitchen blazed through Badger's mind. "Rocket potato! Watch out!" Skunk had said. Badger glanced over his shoulder and saw the potato. Rocket Potato was small, yellow, and now claimed the corner. Badger decided he did not like the look of potatoes in corners, even rocket potatoes.

Rocket Potato

Badger grabbed a muffin from the basket, and was surprised to find it was the last muffin. How many muffins had he eaten? Badger took a bite and chewed. His chewing sounded loud.

Where *exactly* was Skunk?

Badger swallowed and listened.

That's when he heard it—a thumping. The sound came from the second floor.

CHAPTER THREE

THUMP. THUMP.

Skunk! Badger stuffed the muffin into his mouth, swallowed, and pushed back his kitchen chair.

Halfway up the stairs, he heard ripping.

"Flat! Flat! Flat!" came a voice.

This was followed by: *Thump. Thump. Thump.*

A picture came into Badger's mind. He sprinted down the hallway and tossed open the door.

My box room! The room was supposed to be filled with boxes: boxes to the ceiling, boxes wall to wall, teetering towers of boxes that shifted when you tip-clawed in and tip-clawed out. Once there had been a box for every need.

No more. Only a single tower of shoeboxes remained. All of the other boxes lay cut down, flattened, stacked, defeated.

"What are you doing?"

Skunk stopped jumping (*thump*) and grinned at Badger. "I am flattening boxes!"

He grabbed Badger's paw and dragged him into the room. "This room is the perfect room for a skunk!" Skunk pointed at a window seat. "At night I will sit there and look at the moon. When there is not a moon, I will name constellations. I am good at naming constellations. We should go on a night hike, okay?"

Badger nodded, but he was only half listening. He had forgotten what this room looked like before boxes. He did not recall the yellow bed frame. Or the bookcase of books. *A green beanbag chair?*

Skunk wheeled around, arms out wide. He stopped with a stomp. "Tonight I will write Aunt Lula and tell her I have found a room on the second floor."

Badger knew what Aunt Lula would say: "Good! Skunkhas foundaroom!"

Alarmed, Badger said, "What about a box room? You never know when you'll need a box of a certain size."

Skunk turned and stared. "Were you saving these boxes? Oh no. I thought you had not gotten around to emptying this room out, which is why you did not want me to stay on the second floor. I thought, 'These are only boxes. I will flatten them. I will help out.' Boxes take up too much room if you do not keep on top of them." He looked at Badger. "I am sorry."

"What about the Special Guest Closet?" said Badger quickly.

Skunk opened his mouth, closed it, then opened it and said, "I could not stay in the Special Guest Closet for more than one night. Badger, that closet is too small—even for a skunk." Skunk looked around at the piles of flattened boxes. "Do you need this many boxes? Perhaps for rocks? I did not know rocks required so many boxes."

"Of course rocks do not require this many boxes!" Heat rose under Badger's fur.

"Good." Skunk brushed off his paws. "It is time to recycle!" Skunk picked up a stack of flattened boxes and walked them to Badger.

Badger took the stack of boxes. What else could he do? He had read Aunt Lula's letters.

A moment later, Skunk appeared next to him, holding his own stack of flattened boxes. At the top of Skunk's pile were three unflattened shoeboxes. He gave Badger a serious look. "I will find you another box room. I promise." As Skunk left the room, he added, "Recycling feels good. Plus, there are always chickens."

"Chickens?" said Badger. But Skunk was already down the hallway. Curious, Badger followed.

The first chicken appeared as Skunk set down his pile of boxes.

Skunk gave the chicken one of the shoeboxes. "Here you go."

"Bock!" said the chicken, taking the box. The chicken strolled on.

Skunk whispered, "One of the Orpingtons." He raised his eyebrows.

"Yes, well," Badger mumbled. He watched the chicken pick its way down the alley, shoebox under wing, and thought, *Another chicken!*

Badger was setting his pile of boxes down when the next chicken came along. This chicken came at them in herks and jerks, stretching out long yellow legs. Skunk gave the chicken the second shoebox.

"Bock-bock-bockety. Bock-bock!" said the chicken.

Skunk leaned back and howled with laughter. "Good one!"

Together they watched the chicken zig, then zag, then disappear from sight. Skunk smiled at Badger. "Here today, gone to leghorn. That is what I always say. You know?"

Badger did not know, but he nodded anyway. Did chickens live in his neighborhood? *Yesterday—one chicken. Today? Two chickens. That's three chickens*, Badger thought, as he and Skunk bound the piles of flattened boxes together with string and set them beside the recycle bin.

"We have done it!" Skunk clapped his paws.

Badger regarded the piles. No more boxes. No more box room. But then he saw one shoebox on the curb. Badger looked up the alley. He looked down the alley. No chickens.

"A chicken forgot its shoebox," he said to Skunk.

"I saved it," Skunk replied. "For you! It is the best shoebox." He picked it up and held it out.

Badger took it. "Really?" He turned it over in his paws. The lid fit snugly. It had sturdy sides. When you tapped on the box, it sounded pleasingly hollow. "A box like this will hold many things. Thank you!"

Skunk thought a moment. "Hm. That must be why the chickens like shoeboxes too. What do you think chickens keep in shoeboxes?"

Badger laughed. "Har! Eggs?"

Important Rock Work

"Maybe eggs. Chickens do like to collect though."

Eggs reminded Badger of breakfast. Breakfast reminded him of something else: "I'm assuming you will be cleaning the kitchen?"

"Of course not," said Skunk, matter-of-factly. "I cook. You clean. It is a Law of Nature. Anyway, I will be busy moving into the Moon Room."

———◄◊►———

You clean? A Law of Nature? Badger thought as he scrubbed, elbow deep in suds. Meanwhile, Skunk raced up and down the stairs, whistling a tune. Badger scrubbed more and listened to the happy scritch-scratchings of a bristle broom on floorboards. He chipped away at a muffin tin barnacled with batter, while upstairs, the trash bin clanged, furniture scraped across the floor, and something plopped with a reverberating, beanbag-like *POOF*. Skunk's feet pattered in funny, jig-like patterns, and Badger heard him uttering things like, "Yes!" and "This is such a good room!" Badger pulled his paws out of the soapy water and discovered breakfast (eggs, pepper, wet muffin) matted in his fur. He wrote "rubber gloves" on the grocery list, and thought, *Cold cereal in a cold bowl with cold milk has its advantages.*

Meanwhile, a hop-ditty-hop continued upstairs. Was Skunk skipping?

THUMP! Squeaky-squeaky-squeak.

A voice called out, "Did you know this bed is bouncy? It is bouncy."

Badger dried his forearms on a dish towel, and said nothing. He considered the yellow bed frame, the green beanbag chair, and the window seat for observing the moon.

Squeak. Squeak-squeak.

Badger gathered up the smudged, encrusted apron and the moist dish towels and wondered where he would be allowed to keep his boxes. As he tossed the apron and towels into the laundry hamper, he realized he had thanked Skunk for his own shoebox. When Badger had finished cleaning the kitchen, he found himself standing over a small potato lying in the corner. *Rocket Potato.* Skunk had said he would pick it up later.

It will be a test, thought Badger.

He left Rocket Potato in its corner.

———◄�‹○›►———

Badger was sitting in a clean kitchen at a clean kitchen table reading (and re-reading) the same page of *Rock Hound Weekly* when Skunk announced that he'd found a new box room.

Skunk led Badger into the front hallway. "Voila!" he said, opening the folding door and tugging a chain.

The light flickered on and hummed.

"That's my Special Guest Closet," said Badger.

"It is better as a Special Box Closet," said Skunk. "See? I have already put five boxes of different sizes and your new shoebox inside it."

True enough, Skunk had put six boxes, including Badger's shoebox, inside the closet. It was also true that Badger did not have many Special Guests.

"Fine. It's a Special Box Closet," Badger said.

Skunk hopped and grinned. "Good!"

Badger observed Skunk coolly. "Do you like your new room?"

"I do!"

"Good." Badger gave Skunk a stern look. "I am going to do my Important Rock Work now. I am not to be disturbed. Do you understand?"

Skunk nodded.

Badger walked into the kitchen. From the kitchen, he walked directly into his rock room. Someone was behind him. He twisted around. "What?"

Skunk shrugged. "I was seeing where you were going."

Scowling, Badger took hold of one of the pocket doors that separated his rock room from the kitchen and pulled it until it stopped halfway across the room.

Skunk stood, watching him.

"I will need quiet to do Important Rock Work," Badger said. "The pocket doors must remain shut."

"Okay." Skunk nodded again.

Badger walked across the room, took hold of the other pocket door, and pulled it until there was a small gap between the two doors. "Important Rock Work requires concentration and focus."

He stepped through the gap, turned around, and put his face in it. "Do not bother me when I am in the rock room. Got it?"

Skunk's eyes widened. "Got it."

With that, Badger closed the doors.

Then Badger raced across the rock room and closed the door to the hallway. It shut with a satisfying click.

Badger leaned against it to catch his breath and heard Skunk whisper, "Shhh. Rock room." Then he heard *click-click-click* as Skunk tip-clawed away.

CHAPTER FOUR

BADGER DOUBLE-CHECKED: THE POCKET DOORS THAT separated the kitchen from Badger's rock room were shut. The door to the hallway was shut. Skunk was out there. He was in here. Badger closed his eyes, leaned against the hallway door, and despaired. *How will I ever get my Important Rock Work done? I am finished.* His breath came in gulps. His heartbeat ricocheted. Finally he told himself, *You are not finished. Open your eyes.*

So he did. Badger opened his eyes and saw his rock room: There were the bookcases of rocks and the fireplace stacked with geodes. (*Artistic!*) There hung his safety glasses, and over here? His hardness testing kit. Chisels, hammers, saws! Scrapers and tweezers and nailbrushes! Magnifying glasses with wooden handles worn smooth by years of Important Rock Work. And in the center of the room? Badger's rock table, his rock light, his rock stool.

The rock room is mine. Badger's eyes widened with relief. *Yes—mine.*

He tip-clawed over to the rock table and switched the rock light on. The light pooled on the table and illuminated an object. The object had pink and gray specks. Some of the specks sparkled.

He rubbed his paws together, then gently pulled out his rock stool and sat down.

He picked the object up. It felt weighty. He brought it close, and whispered, "Rock or mineral?"

"Rock or mineral" was *always* the first question. Even if Badger thought he knew the answer, he began at the beginning–the *very* beginning. He asked the first question. There'd be time for tests and prying. Eventually, Badger would scrape and scratch: Did the object leave a streak on the white porcelain tile? A streak of what color? Later, the name would be divulged, uncovered. Sometimes it took a drop of acid. (Fizzing! A carbonate!) Other times the pass of Badger's paw over the object's surface caused a sedimentary crumbling. Tools were kept at the ready: magnifying glasses and a microscope, a blowpipe and a Bunsen burner, gloves and safety goggles. There was a bradawl, a tiny spatula, brushes of all sizes, and a fine dust blower (which Badger had nicknamed his "puffer").

But first–before *any* of this–there was the beginning. There was the asking of the first question. Badger liked the beginning. At the beginning, he cleared the clutter of assumptions and guesses from his mind. He opened himself up to any possibility, and asked the question.

"Rock or mineral?" Badger said.

Yes, the beginning was one of Badger's favorite moments.

"Mineral or rock? . . . Rock? Mineral? Hmm . . ." Badger turned the rock over and over under the light. Minerals were made of one basic material–one element or "an elemental compound," as the rock scientists said. There tended to be a sameness about a mineral. A rock, though, was a combination–a combination of minerals, or a combination of rocks and minerals. Two minerals stuck together? That would be a rock. Five minerals mixed up and a rock glommed together in a mass? Also, a rock.

The object in front of Badger had a gray speckle. It also had a pink speckle. Additionally, there was that speckle that sparkled.

Badger stood up and circled, his eye on the object in the pool of light on his rock table. He stopped mid-step. Then he hopped in front of the object, tapped a speckle–"Huh"–and stared. He circled again. He scratched his head and stopped. He stuck a claw in the air. "Ah!" He thought and then sighed, chuckled and shook his head. "No, no, no."

Suddenly, Badger rushed the table, grabbed hold of the object, and tossed it into the air.

The object flew up.

The object flew down.

Badger caught it, and with all his might, he yelled out the answer: "ROCK!"

Badger always answered the first question with a yell. This was usual. What was not usual was the pitter-patter of feet that followed.

The door to the hallway burst open. "Are you okay? You yelled 'rock'!"

There stood Skunk.

Badger groaned. He dropped to his rock stool.

Skunk stepped into Badger's rock room.

Badger set the rock on the table. It clunked.

"Badger? You yelled?" Skunk came closer.

"Did I?" Badger mumbled, rubbing his face with his paws.

"Yes, you did. You yelled 'rock' loudly!" Skunk walked up to his rock table, and pointed at the pink-and-gray rock. "Is this the rock? Yes, that is probably the rock. You were staring at that one."

"Rock or mineral," Badger mumbled.

Skunk blinked at him, and pointed again. "That is a pink-and-gray rock."

"A mineral is–" Badger started.

"Something in breakfast cereal?" Skunk interrupted. "Yes, I know! There is a lot of breakfast cereal in the cupboard. I have learned that cereal boxes like to tell you about minerals– minerals, minerals, minerals! Why do they do that? Minerals do not sound tasty to me. Listen, if that is the troublesome rock, you should get rid of it. Troublesome rocks are not worth the trouble, if you do not mind me saying so. Rocks are hard."

Badger closed his eyes.

"Badger?"

Badger opened his eyes, sighed, and looked at Skunk. "Skunk, you must let me do my Important Rock Work. When these doors are closed, you must leave me alone. I must not see you. I must not hear you. Do you understand?"

Skunk's jaw dropped. "But you yelled 'rock'! If you hear me yell 'rock,' I would appreciate it if you came quickly."

"If I yell 'rock,' leave me alone."

"That is concerning. But okay."

Skunk stood there. Instead of leaving, he leaned closer and frowned in concentration at Badger. "How about some chamomile tea? Chamomile is a soothing, *smoothing* tea. You look prickly, Badger."

"Goodbye," said Badger.

Skunk nodded to himself. "Yes, perhaps it is too late for chamomile." He gave Badger a last look and finally said, "Goodbye."

The door to the hallway clicked shut.

Badger sighed. He breathed in. *I have made my point.* He breathed out. *I have said what needed to be said.* He breathed in. *Surely, there will be no more problems.*

The pocket doors popped open. An eyeball appeared!

Badger jumped.

Skunk stuck his head through. "What about lunch?"

"No lunch!"

Skunk looked worried. "You will be hungry. Lunch is the second-best meal of the day."

"I will not be hungry! Do not disturb me!"

"Okay." Skunk pulled his head back through the opening, and shoved the pocket doors closed.

Badger's head fell to his rock table and thunked.

Many, many minutes passed.

Finally, Badger sat up, rubbed his forehead, and picked up the pink-and-gray rock.

"You are a rock," he whispered to the rock.

He glanced at the pocket doors separating his rock room from the kitchen. He glanced at the door to the hallway. He expected to hear footsteps coming closer and to see the slight jiggle of the door handle.

Badger waited. The door handle did not jiggle. He heard no sounds. *Awfully quiet out there*, he thought.

He stood up and went over to the bookcase to retrieve his hardness testing kit, and thought of Skunk. *Always hopping, thumping, frolicking about.* Badger set out his white porcelain tile, his penny, his chunk of glass, and the talc in a row and listened closely to the sounds in the brownstone. There was not a patter or a floorboard squeak, or the clatter of kitchen utensils. Where was Skunk? What was Skunk doing? Badger's heartbeat sped up.

Ukulele! Badger straightened. He imagined Skunk in his room, opening his closet, and finding the ukulele. Badger's eyes grew large, then darted.

Stop! he told himself firmly. *Maybe it is quiet because Skunk is reading a book.* There was an entire bookcase of books in Skunk's room. *Or perhaps Skunk is taking a nap.*

No—not possible! Skunk told animals to tuck napkins in here and sit there. With Skunk in the room, potatoes flew from pans and sheltered in corners. Peppers were set on fire—on fire! These were not the habits of the napping book reader.

Badger stepped toward the hallway door. He needed to check his bedroom.

Sit down—Important Rock Work! he told himself.

Badger went back to his rock table and sat down.

Ukulele! Badger thought and stood up.

That was when the back door slammed. This was followed by a whistled tune and the crumple of a paper sack set on the counter.

Skunk had gone out and returned.

Oh, thought Badger.

Then, clear as a bell, Badger heard Skunk whisper, "Badger is working. Must be quiet—shhh."

Badger sat down with a groan. He ran a paw through his stripe and thought, *This cannot continue—enough is enough.* Then he sharpened his favorite pencil, and opened his field notebook to a fresh page. He wrote:

Dear Aunt Lula,

   Skunk has arrived. He is lively. He bounces. He skips. He whistles tunes and clangs pans.

Unfortunately, concentration shatters when doors are knocked upon and proclamations are loudly delivered. When eyeballs appear unexpectedly between pocket doors, one jumps out of one's seat!

Therefore, after a short visit, Skunk will have to make his home elsewhere. I know you will understand, as you often speak glowingly of my Important Rock Work.

On the precipice of an Important Rock Discovery,

Badger

Badger ripped the page from the notebook, and folded it into an envelope. He addressed the envelope, stuck on the United Pelican stamp, and set the letter on the corner of his rock table. Then he went back to work.

With the letter on his table, Badger did not mind the noises coming from the kitchen when Skunk made his lunch and then later, his dinner. Badger's stomach rumbled when something sizzled in a fry pan and a pleasing smell drifted through the pocket doors, but he patted the envelope and worked on.

When he had solved his rock, Badger left the brownstone with the letter. He shut the front door noiselessly and then trotted down the front steps and along the sidewalk to the United

Pelican mailbox. He opened the mailbox lid and dropped his letter inside.

That takes care of that, Badger thought as the mailbox clanged shut.

With a spring in his step, Badger turned and headed back to the brownstone.

CHAPTER FIVE

BADGER FOUND THE BROWNSTONE QUIET ON HIS RETURN from mailing the letter. *Skunk must be out,* he thought.

His stomach roared. He rushed to the kitchen. His left paw found the cereal cupboard, while the right one pulled open the utensil drawer. The cereal box hit the counter. The spoon clattered beside it. The milk landed (*chunk*), along with a bowl (*clunk*).

Badger stood and ate. His spoon clinked the bowl, slid across the bottom, and rose to Badger's mouth. *Clink-slide-slurp, clink-slide-slurp, clink-slide-slurp.*

Eating ended, as cereal-eating always did, with Badger holding an empty box. *Shake, shake? Shake?* As cereal dust rained onto the puddle of milk in his bowl, words surfaced in Badger's mind: *Cold cereal in a cold bowl with cold milk.* Badger tapped his spoon against the side of the bowl in time with the words: *Cold cereal (tap) in a cold bowl (tap, tap) with cold milk (tap).*

Badger remembered the breakfast Skunk had prepared for him: breakfast hot chocolate, warm strawberry cinnamon muffins, eggs with roasted peppers.

"Mmmm . . . mmm," he mumbled.

He held the empty cereal box in front of him and read, "Fruity-O's Cereal! Fortified with minerals and vitamins!" Skunk was right. Minerals and vitamins did not sound tasty.

Badger wrote "No more Fruity-O's" on the refrigerator grocery list and decided he would go to bed early.

On the way to his bedroom, Badger heard a sound coming from the old box room.

The door was ajar. Badger pushed the door to peek in and inhaled sharply.

In a spot of lamplight, Skunk sat curled in the green beanbag chair with an enormous book open on his lap. Light from a reading lamp pooled on the book's pages. Across the room, moonlight streamed through the window onto a window seat lined with plump, mismatched pillows.

Moon Room, thought Badger.

The Moon Room

Skunk rubbed his eyes. "Hello, Badger."

"You're here." Badger said this in not the nicest way. Then he realized that he had not even knocked.

Skunk did not appear to notice. "Yes, I am here. It is Long Story Night. You sound like a polka when you eat cereal." Skunk held up a big book. "Have you read this story? It is called *Henry V*. Henry V is a king with a short last name."

I sound like a polka when I eat cereal? Badger tried to look as if this did not bother him and stepped closer to read the big book's cover. It read: *Henry V* by William Shakespeare.

He shook his head. "No—that isn't a book about rocks."

Skunk scooted to the edge of the beanbag chair and sat upright. "You should read this. *Henry V* is about two kings who are in a battle. It is an upsetting story, but a good one for Long Story Night, and King Henry says interesting things. For instance, King Henry says that the fastest way to win a kingdom is by being kind and gentle instead of using violence and cruelty. Do you think that is true? I do not know what I think at all. I am not even sure I trust Henry V! He is a king. He got everybody into a battle. Battles are not gentle and kind! But I would like to know what you think. What do you think, Badger?"

Skunk waited.

"Ah. Hmm," Badger muttered. He was not used to this kind of question—especially at night after eating an entire box of cereal.

Skunk ran his claw down the page, and tapped. "He actually says this: '. . . when lenity and cruelty play for a kingdom, the gentler gamester is the soonest winner.' Does that help?"

Skunk looked up and waited.

"Huh," said Badger. He thought about it one way, and then another. His thoughts dead-ended, so he backed them out and tried another direction. "Maybe? I hope so?"

Skunk sighed and nodded. "Yes, 'hope' seems right to me. Gentle and kind is the way I would *like* the world to be. I *hope* it will be that way. But Badger, if it were true that kindness and gentleness were the best way to win a kingdom—or win anything at all—wouldn't everyone do it? Not everyone is gentle and kind. Even I myself find it hard to be kind and gentle. Sometimes I get mad. Also, I am a small animal, and being small is difficult. Sometimes I wish I had a grizzly bear arm to swat, or an alligator mouth to clack. But instead, I am a skunk." He looked at his tail. "Even when no one is hurt, you get chased out of town. That does not feel like you are 'the soonest winner.'"

Badger looked at Skunk's tail with some alarm. "You do not use *that*, ah, willy-nilly?"

"Oh no, of course not. I would only spray in the direst of circumstances." Skunk smiled. "Thank you, Badger. It helped to talk." He put his paw in the book and closed it. "Did you figure out your troublesome rock?"

Badger nodded. "Tourmaline pegmatite."

"Oh. Is that its name?"

"Yes," said Badger with a chuckle.

"Well then, tomorrow I would like to hear the story of tourmaline pegmatite," said Skunk. "I have not heard a lot of rock stories."

"You would?"

"Yes, I would," said Skunk. "Rocks are close-lipped, unlike oysters. Rocks do not speak much, except for the rocks in the rock shaker. Those rocks chatter, chatter, chatter, but that is because of the shaker. Also, I have not learned how to speak 'rock.'"

"Rock tumbler," corrected Badger with a smile on his lips. "Tomorrow I will tell you a rock story."

"Good." Then Skunk opened his big book and began again to read.

———◄o►———

That night, as Badger got into his pajamas and slipped into bed, he thought about Skunk and the letter he'd sent to Aunt Lula.

48

He had to admit that talking to Skunk had been an enjoyable way to end the evening. *It would never work out! But Skunk certainly has his moments.*

Head on the pillow with his eyes shut, Badger replayed the sounds he had made while eating cereal—*clink-slide-slurp, clink-slide-slurp, clink-slide-slurp*—and laughed, "Har!"

I do *sound like a polka!*

With a smile on his face, Badger fell asleep.

———◁◦▷———

The next morning Badger awoke to a yell: "Onion and mushroom omelets! Warm rhubarb muffins! Breakfast hot chocolate coming soon!"

"Breakfast hot chocolate," mumbled Badger. He rolled out of bed, stepped free of the covers, and bounded down the stairs.

Skunk's second breakfast was as delicious as the first one.

"Mmmm . . . mm . . . Mahmahmah," mumbled Badger as he chewed. Badger wrapped his paw around the last rhubarb muffin and offered to do the dishes.

Skunk stopped cold. "Are you sure? Dirty dishes make you mad."

"You cook, I clean. Isn't that the deal?" said Badger, ignoring the look Skunk was giving him.

Skunk peered up at him. "It *is* a big job to make breakfast. It *is* fair. But there are a lot of dishes." Skunk gestured at the countertop with an egg-covered whisk. The words *teetering, heaped,* and *glop* came to mind. Also, Badger noticed that Rocket Potato remained in Rocket Potato Corner.

But none of this bothered Badger one whit. The letter had been mailed. What was done was done. Would it hurt him to clean the kitchen a couple more times?

Badger shrugged casually. "It's only fair."

Skunk looked at Badger sideways, blinked, then nodded. "Okay. But I will help. It is easier if someone dries."

"You will?"

"I will."

So Badger washed and Skunk dried. They talked about things Skunk liked: good storybooks, a farmers' market he'd found, and—spoken in a hush—"the Milky Way." They talked about things Badger liked: rocks, minerals, and how agates formed in volcano gas bubbles. ("Lava bubbles!" said Skunk, with a hop. "Er . . . not exactly," said Badger.)

But then Skunk began to pace back and forth. He twiddled spoons, then forks. He flicked his dish towel against the kitchen cabinets (*swap-swap-swap*). He took a long look at Badger, opened his mouth, and closed it again.

Finally he said, "Badger?"

The bowl Badger held slipped from his paw, splashed into the soapy water, and clunked. "Sludge and slurry! What?"

Skunk swatted the floor with his towel (*swap!*), and said in a burst, "Sometimes I get excited and do things." He looked up. "Badger, I am sorry about your box room. I should have asked before I stomped on boxes. I did think I was helping, and empty boxes remind me of bubble wrap. I never thought that maybe you liked your boxes puffy. I am sorry."

"It's okay," Badger said.

Skunk crossed his arms. "You were mad! I know I am right about that!"

Badger tried to remember how he felt before he'd sent the letter to Aunt Lula. He frowned, then remembered: "Yes, I was mad. But now? I'm not mad." Badger smiled and patted Skunk on the back.

Skunk beamed. "That is good news!"

Then Skunk pointed a claw at Badger. "You said you remembered Aunt Lula mentioning me, but it did not seem like you expected a skunk. It seemed like I was a shock. Is that true?"

Badger sagged against the sink with a little smile. "I hadn't read Aunt Lula's letters."

"You said . . . !"

"I did."

"You did not know I was coming!"

Badger shook his head. "I did not know you were coming."

"That explains everything." Skunk grinned. "You should read Aunt Lula's letters!"

"I will–believe me."

"Ha!"

"Har!"

Skunk plucked up a fork and they got back to work cleaning the kitchen.

———◄o►———

Kitchen cleaned and a successful morning's rock work done–*No interruptions! Rock identified! Finished early!*–Badger joined Skunk for lunch.

"You know," said Skunk, poking the air with a pickled asparagus spear, "it is quite chickmopolitan here. I have seen a Blue Booted Bantam, two Silkies, three Javas walking with a Ko Shamo, and lots of chickens I did not even know. I met chickens from South America–real travelers! You are lucky to live here. The chickens said they did not know you, but you were probably tolerable as a roommate. They are hoping that if I am your roommate you will turn off the rock shaker. They think I will not like the rock shaker. Badger, the rock shaker is loud."

"Tumbler," Badger corrected. "It *is* loud. Yes." He scraped at his baked potato, making sure to get some olives and sun-dried tomatoes. Then he frowned. "The chickens call me 'tolerable'?"

Skunk chewed his asparagus spear and swallowed. "With chickens, tolerable is good. Chickens get a lot of trouble. You will like the chickens. So down-to-earth! By the way, did you meet a chicken? A Dominicker said she startled you. She said you were one of those animals that did not expect chickens to speak."

Badger thought back to the gray-and-white-speckled chicken he had seen two days ago. Was he really supposed to say "bock"?

Skunk leaned over the table. "Would you like to meet the chickens?"

"Yes," said Badger, and he realized he meant it.

Skunk clapped his paws. "Good, good, good."

"Now," said Skunk, leaning back with a biscuit in his paw. "Tell me the story of the Touring Pegmatic Rock."

"Tourmaline pegmatite begins with fire, lava, and magma deep inside our Earth," Badger began.

"Fire, lava, magma," repeated Skunk. He leaned his chin on a paw, took a bite of biscuit, and listened.

———◅◦▻———

Afterwards, Skunk asked Badger to show him on a map, so they cleared the kitchen table and Badger spread out one of his geological survey maps. Side by side—Skunk on a chair, Badger beside the chair—they leaned over the map. Badger told Skunk how he used maps on rock-finding expeditions.

Skunk gasped. "Rock-finding *expedition*? *What* is that?"

Badger explained about how he camped out—

"Under the stars?" interrupted Skunk.

"Technically yes, but—"

"With a picnic every day?" interrupted Skunk again.

"I guess. I do eat outside."

Skunk hopped from one foot to the other. "What else? What else?"

So Badger explained how clues in the landscape led to a particular rock.

Skunk slapped his paw on the map. "Like X marks the spot?"

"Sort of . . . yes."

Then Skunk turned and said, "Badger, what are we waiting for?"

"Har!" laughed Badger, because that's exactly how he felt too.

———◄○►———

That afternoon, Skunk set off to explore North Twist and Badger did the lunch dishes. Badger didn't mind doing the dishes by himself. He'd had a terrific day. Badger even smiled at Rocket Potato (which he left cradled in Rocket Potato Corner).

Suddenly, Badger remembered the letter he had sent to Aunt Lula. He stood frozen in the middle of the kitchen floor and thought. He thought for one second . . . for two seconds . . . for three seconds. Finally, Badger snapped himself out of it: *Surely, it is for the best! How could this living arrangement ever work out?*

When the kitchen was clean, Badger took the latest copy of *Rock Hound Weekly* up to his bedroom. He would see if one of his rock discoveries had made it into print.

———◄○►———

Several hours later, Badger awoke with his face smashed on top of his *Weekly*. He sat up, folded the newspaper, and set it on his desk. Two of his rock discoveries had been written up! He planned to clip the articles out and store them in his publication file.

Then Badger realized it was quiet. *Very quiet.* He went downstairs to investigate. Skunk was not in the kitchen. Instead, Badger found a note on the table. It read:

Badger,

I will be back after dinner. <u>Do not go anywhere tonight</u>. There will be a surprise!

Skunk

A surprise? Badger read it again. It said "surprise."

Badger's eyes widened. He read the note a third time.

"Oh," said Badger, wiping at his eyes with the back of a paw. It had been a long, long time since someone had prepared a surprise for him.

Badger felt a sharp ping. *Maybe I should not have written that letter?*

But there was a surprise coming, so Badger pushed the thought aside.

A surprise! He could not wait.

CHAPTER SIX

BADGER DID NOT WAIT LONG FOR THE SURPRISE. FIRST came a sound.

It was an awful sound. Badger thought a tiny elephant had gotten stuck in one of his ears. It trumpeted! Badger jumped and pounded the right side of his head. He pounded the left. Then Badger realized the trumpeting wasn't *in* his ears. Groaning, he followed the sound out of the kitchen and down the front hallway, and jerked open the front door.

Skunk stood on the stoop's landing with his back to Badger. He blew into an orange stick.

Skunk turned around and removed the stick from his mouth. "Hello, Badger!"

The sound exited Badger's ears like corks forced from bottles. *Pup! EeeePUP!* Badger crumpled onto the stone parapet and panted, rubbing his ears.

Skunk pocketed the stick and skidded to the edge of the stoop. He held a paw over his eyes, surveying the neighborhood. "Any minute now! Any minute any minute any minute."

Badger followed Skunk's gaze, expecting to see red-faced neighbors also massaging their ears. But no neighbors appeared. In fact, the neighborhood looked as it always looked: meadow across the street, sidewalk to the mailbox, brownstones lined up like dominoes ascending Queggly Hill.

Skunk leapt and pointed to the south. "Ahoy! Orloff!"

Badger saw an odd, upright bird with feathered breeches.

Skunk leaned toward Badger and whispered, "Named after the Russian count Alexei Grigoryevich Orlov. But she is not Russian—she is Iranian."

Badger stood to get a better look. With every step the Orloff took, feathers shook (muffs, cowls, beard, and shaggy eyebrows). The Orloff slowly turned. Badger felt appraised (left-right, left-right). Then the Orloff fluffed her feathers, stuck her beak in the air, and made a sharp cry, "Rrrrr-RR!"

"What kind of bird is that?" Badger asked.

"Chicken! Chickens are the only ones who hear the chicken whistle," Skunk replied.

Badger thought of the orange stick and blinked. "You don't hear anything when you blow it? Not even a little?"

"Of course not—I am not a chicken."

A badger is not a chicken! Badger thought. Badger would have said something but Skunk hopped and pointed. "Look! Over there! And there!"

"Oh!" Badger's jaw went slack. The landscape had gone chicken. Under, over, behind—chickens. Across the street, in the park, near the mailbox—chickens. The wattles! The combs! The bright red faces! Oblongs, rounds, tiny, and shrub-sized. ("Jersey Giant," said Skunk.) There were chickens strolling on stork legs. ("Three Ko Shamos on the right!" said Skunk.) Chickens wearing bell-bottoms, plumed berets, and flippers, all made of feathers. The chickens came in colors. *A purple chicken?* Some were mottled, some speckled, and some sparkled. Everywhere Badger looked, the earth moved with a chicken beat, syncopated in herks and jerks, and this eye, then that eye, then *step-step-step, peer-PECK!*

On the brownstone stoop, Badger swayed on his feet. "Are these *all* chickens?"

"Hen chickens," said Skunk, misunderstanding him. "Hens get things done. Hens work together. I do not like to speak ill of a chicken, but Badger, too many roosters are trouble. A rooster wants all the attention. A rooster fights and claws and pecks. Some roosters do not know when to stop cock-a-doodle-doo-ing! Even the hens think it is best to keep roosters to a minimum. I did tell Larry, though. Larry is different."

Badger pointed at a group of four fleshy, sunbaked birds and crossed his arms. "*Those* are turkeys."

"Chickens–Transylvania Naked Neck chickens, Badger."

Then Badger noticed that the chickens–*all* of them–were coming closer. *Step-peer-peck.*

And closer. *Step-peer-peck.*

And closer! *Step-peer. Step-step. Peck!*

Badger stumbled backwards and clutched at the stone of the house. "Triassic-Jurassic sandstone," he mumbled out of habit, his thoughts firmly on the approaching chicken tidal wave.

Skunk rushed into the sea of feathers. "Hello! Hello!" he yelled. "So nice to meet you!"

Badger watched Skunk greet chicken after chicken. Then the Orloff stepped up and apparently told some sort of joke.

"Orange foot *who*?" Badger heard Skunk say.

The landscape had gone chicken.

"Bockety bock-bock, bockety-bockety-bock-bock?" said the Orloff.

"Ha! Did you hear that, Badger?"

Badger had heard. "Bock bock?" Not that funny. Badger shrugged.

The chickens gathered around Skunk turned their gaze on Badger (one eye, the other eye).

"Bock," said a tiny orange ball of feathers.

"Bock-bock," said a speckled brown job.

"BBBooock-bock-bock," said the Orloff.

Skunk looked briefly at Badger, then turned to the chickens. "You are right. I do not think Badger understands your dialect."

"What dialect?" Badger huffed.

Skunk gave Badger a concerned look.

The chickens conferred. The speckled brown job said, "Bock! Bock-bockety-bock."

Skunk waved his paws. "No, he is smart enough. Badger knows a lot about rocks."

Badger gasped. "*Smart enough?* For *chickens?*"

"Shhh!" said Skunk. "You will speak clearly in no time at all–I promise. The chickens will like you, and you will like the chickens. Chickens are good to know."

Then—to Badger's horror—Skunk pushed past him and opened the brownstone door. "Storytime!" he yelled.

"Wait!" said Badger. But it was too late. Chickens rushed for the door with the force of a pressure hose.

—◁○▷—

It had happened so quickly.

Badger and Skunk stood in the doorway of Badger's rock room and gawked. In one flick of a chicken head, the rock room had been overthrown in a chicken coop *d'état*. This wasn't Badger's rock room, this was the Wild West of Chicken, the Saloon at Dead-bug End, the Last Stand at Corncob Corral. The chickens chattered, and then burst forth in a SQUAWK and a clap of wings. The ones that flew took to the air. Some of these chickens perched on the chandelier, which now swung like a swing set.

Badger's mouth opened and closed, opened and closed.

Skunk glanced at him. "I do not usually get this many chickens," he explained. "The most until now was sixteen. That was once—only once." Skunk looked at Badger and kept talking: "I did not know that chickens liked rock rooms." He added, "Usually they go into the kitchen first." Skunk peeked at Badger and hastily looked away. "Yes, chickens continually surprise!"

"Surprise," mumbled Badger.

Skunk kept talking: "But after you have blown the chicken whistle it would be rude not to invite them in for a story."

Badger thrust a paw toward the chicken outbreak in his rock room. "Rude? What about this?"

Skunk nodded. "It is good that rocks are hard."

Then Skunk froze. "Oh dear," he said softly.

Badger turned. "What?"

Skunk gave Badger a swift smile. "You do not have any gravel, do you?"

"Why?"

"Chickens eat gravel. Digestive aid. Or so chickens say."

"Gravel is *rock*. Chickens *eat* rocks?" Badger took in the bookshelves filled with boxes of rocks, the rock table, the fireplace mantel—all covered in chickens.

Skunk took one look at Badger and said, "I will make the popcorn!"

"AaaaaRRRUUUGH," roared Badger, as he careened into chickens.

Skunk popped popcorn. Badger shut, boxed up, and locked. He growled continually.

Badger ended up spread over his rock table, clamped to his rock stool, batting at the Jersey Giant who seemed determined to perch on the gooseneck of Badger's rock light. When the Jersey Giant finally gave up, Badger let his head plop on the table.

Badger stayed like this until Skunk clunked a bowl of popcorn in front of him.

"For sustenance. You have wilted," said Skunk.

Badger lifted his head in time to see Skunk, bearing bowls of popcorn, disappear into a whirlwind of chickens.

Badger took a paw-full of popcorn, chewed, and sat up.

He grabbed another paw-full. Then another. That's when he saw her. The tiny orange ball of feathers stood next to his pencil mug.

Badger began to spit-polish his rock light, watching her out of the corner of his eye. A yellow foot appeared from the poof of feathers. It extended out, out slo-oow-ly. Quick as a wink, she set the foot down, lowered the other yellow foot beside it, and poofed out her feathers. He put his head next to her tiny poof body. "I'm smart," he growled.

The ball of feathers pecked—hard.

"Ow!" said Badger, patting his snout.

"Bock-bock," said the poof of feathers. She slowly extended her head out of the orange feathers and stared (left-right-left, blink, blink). Then she did a two-step, two-step, two-step toward Badger's popcorn. "Bock!"

"Har!" Badger laughed. He reached into the bowl and put a piece of popcorn in front of her. Then he sat back and watched.

The tiny orange hen barely gave him a glance. She stepped up and ate the corn. "Bock."

Badger set another piece of popcorn in front of her. "I do rock *science*."

"Bock-bock," said the tiny orange hen, pecking at the popcorn.

Badger got a big paw-full and set it in front of her. "Rock science takes persistence, determination, and character. Also, you have to be very, very, *very* smart."

"Bock-bock-bock-bock." The tiny orange hen tossed a piece of popcorn back and gulped.

Badger ate several more paw-fulls of popcorn. When Badger saw that the tiny orange hen had finished eating hers, he reached for a paw-full.

"Bock!"

Badger stopped mid-reach.

"Bock!" said the hen again. Badger saw two tiny eyes peer up at him (right eye, left eye, right eye). Then the tiny orange hen hopped into the crook of one of Badger's arms.

So light, thought Badger.

The tiny orange hen sighed, tucked her beak under her wing, and went to sleep.

"Oh," said Badger.

"Cockle-EH-eck. Eck. ECK."

A grizzled rooster rose stiffly from the geodes in the fireplace. The bird looked partially plucked.

Larry? thought Badger.

"Thank you, Larry," came Skunk's voice.

Badger turned and saw Skunk sitting on the floor, holding a book with an embroidered cover.

"BoooOOOOck . . . boooock, boooock," the chickens murmured. The tiny orange hen stirred and adjusted herself in Badger's arms.

Skunk opened the book. "Chicken Little the Mighty," he read.

He paused, then looked directly at Badger. "To catch you up: Something fell from above onto Chicken Little. It was only something like a leaf, but it frightened Chicken Little and she jumped to the biggest possible conclusion. 'The sky is falling! The sky is falling!' she told everyone. A lot of other birds believed her. Those birds followed Chicken Little straight into the den of Foxy Loxy! Luckily, Chicken Little and her friends escaped unharmed, but Chicken Little's reputation was ruined."

Skunk turned to the book. He began to read, his voice filling the room. As Badger listened, the story seemed to unfold in front of him.

It went like this:

Humbled by the Sky-Is-Falling Fiasco, Chicken Little left on a journey. She was determined to make up for what she had done. "I will not return until I find Something That Makes a Difference," Chicken Little said.

It was quite a journey! Chicken Little traveled through bands of starlings that leapt from the leaf litter and frogs that chorused to lead her astray. She snuck past lines of battling army ants and hid in damp ditches. Finally, she met a wise green parakeet. The parakeet gave her a magic kernel of corn. "Eat the kernel in a Time of Need," the parakeet told her.

Traversing the mountain glacier, Chicken Little lost a claw to frostbite. Then a crust of snow gave way with nothing but air underneath it. It was a crevasse, a crack in the glacier, half hidden by blown-over snow. Into the crevasse, Chicken Little fell! She turned in the air, falling, falling. In desperation she flapped the wings that she'd been told were worthless.

The wings worked!

Or well enough. Chicken Little skidded onto the other side of the crevasse and dug her remaining claws into the crusty snow.

The effort about did her in. Chicken Little lay on the ice panting, trying to remember which pocket held her magic corn kernel. Where was it? She could not seem to find it! And here, Chicken Little faced several facts: Bantam hens were not made for mountaineering. Also, a chicken on ice is soon a dead chicken. If it were not for a family of mountain pikas dragging her into their warm straw-filled den, Chicken Little would be no more. The pikas saved Chicken Little's life. In return, Chicken Little left the pikas three eggs.

"The eggs confused the pikas. Pikas are small rabbits, and only eat plants. What would they do with three big eggs? There is a story about what happened to the eggs, which we should tell another time," said Skunk.

"BOCK!" said the Jersey Giant.

"Okay, okay . . . Back to the story," said Skunk.

Later, Chicken Little would be grateful that she had not used her magic kernel of corn on the glacier. If she had used it on that glacier it would have served only her. By waiting, Chicken Little was able to use it for the . . .

". . . Greater Good of All Chickens!" said Skunk.

More adventures followed. Chicken Little traveled further, and farther . . . and further.

Use the kernel! Use the kernel! Badger thought again and again.

Then one day, Chicken Little saw a figure at the far end of a windless lake. It was a woman in hiking shoes and a herringbone-check wool blazer with patches on the elbows. Chicken Little saw the woman write in the sand with her walking stick.

When Chicken Little arrived at the lake's far end, the woman was gone, but her markings in the sand were still there.

It was Chicken Scratch! Yes, that most ancient of chicken languages—words, numbers, symbols. Chicken Little read, "Electron, energy, exponent . . . wave number, unit length, integer . . . electromagnetic radiation in a vacuum . . . principal quantum numbers of the orbitals . . . The Constant!" There were symbols too—divided and multiplied by, infinity, greater than, less than, equal to, coefficients, decimals.

That sounds like a mathematical equation! thought Badger. He nearly dropped the tiny orange hen.

That night, Chicken Little considered what she had read in the sand.

The next morning, Chicken Little knew that if she could apply the chicken scratch, it would be Something That Made a Difference. Chicken Little gobbled down the magic corn kernel. That is how she brought back . . .

"The Quantum Leap!" said Skunk. "The Quantum Leap is not a leap, or a hop, or a hurdling, but a *disappearance* in one place and a *reappearance* in another. The Quantum Leap made the chickens' world safer. Chicken Little became known as Chicken Little the Mighty!"

That's how they do it? Science? thought Badger, looking around at the chickens in wonder.

Skunk closed the book with a thump. "THE END."

The chickens broke into squawks. "Bock!" "Bock-bock!"

The tiny orange hen in Badger's arms tapped him with her beak. Badger nodded at her.

That was a good story, he thought, sighing. Adventure and science made the best stories. Now he looked around his rock room. There were chickens on the floor, chickens on the bookshelves, chickens on the rock tumbler and the windowsills.

He looked at the tiny orange hen in his arms. *Orange like an agate*, he thought, and happiness flooded through him.

This is the best night of my life.

A speckled chicken popped and fluttered. "Bock-bock-bock!"

With that, Badger's rock room drained of chickens. The tiny orange hen scrabbled from Badger's arms and plunged into the burbling, feathered surge.

Badger looked at Skunk.

Skunk grinned. He gestured to Badger to follow.

Badger followed.

The moon!

The moon filled the porch end to end.

"Oh," said Badger.

Skunk sighed.

For a long while, Badger and Skunk stood side by side on the porch watching the moon rise. The chickens had gathered in the yard. Badger's dried-out garden bloomed with feathery poofs and tufts, crowns and tassels.

"Chickens are beautiful," whispered Badger.

Skunk nodded. "Yes. But there are at least one hundred chickens. That is too many chickens. In North Twist, I will have to be careful with my chicken whistle."

"Har!" laughed Badger.

"Ha!" laughed Skunk.

Without warning, the chickens shook themselves off, formed a line, and strolled past Skunk and Badger into the brownstone.

Badger looked at Skunk.

Skunk shrugged. "There is popcorn left."

Then Skunk sneezed. Colors burst off Skunk's nose like fireworks.

"Oh!" Badger stepped back.

Skunk smiled and rubbed his nose. "Moon dust gets everywhere."

Skunk pointed at Badger's face. "Eyebrows." Then Skunk followed the chickens inside.

Badger rubbed a paw over his eyebrows and swore he saw a dust—a dust with a shimmer—drift in front of his eyes. As he entered the brownstone again, Badger thought he could not remember a more magical evening.

The doorbell rang.

"I'll get it!" yelled Skunk.

CHAPTER SEVEN

"STOOOOAAAAAAT!" YELLED SKUNK.

At the word *stoat*, chickens jumped and climbed. They scrambled onto bookshelves. They scooted behind rocks. Chickens tucked themselves under cushions and clambered into cupboards. The air fogged with chicken dander and wobbled with feathers.

Badger ran toward the front door. Skunk was running back toward the kitchen. The two of them collided in the hallway.

"UngGUH."

"Ow!"

Then everything went still—so still that Badger heard feathers hitting the floorboards.

Skunk looked at Badger with eyes gone wild. He pointed at the door. "Stoat-gram *for you*. Who would send a stoat-gram? What were they thinking? I slammed the door shut!"

The doorbell rang.

Badger nodded resolutely. "I will get it."

Skunk ran in front of him. "Leave it. That is a stoat. Stoats are *not friendly*!"

Badger stepped around him.

Skunk grabbed Badger's forearm and hissed, "Badger, there are *chickens* here."

"I will not invite the stoat in," said Badger, as he freed himself from Skunk's paw.

Skunk's jaw dropped in horror. He looked around. Then he slapped his paws to his mouth. "Hide!" he yelled, and raced around the corner.

The doorbell rang-rang-RAAAAANG again. Badger went to the door thinking, *It is only a stoat.* Badgers were bigger.

He opened the door. *A stoat on the job*, thought Badger as he looked down upon the stoat, observing her messenger bag and the SPEEDY STOAT DELIVERY patch sewn on her company jacket.

"Looking for a badger named Badger. Heh. Descriptive. You that particular badger?" asked the stoat.

Badger nearly rolled his eyes, but stopped himself. "That's me. Got a stoat-gram for me?"

"Right here, right here," mumbled the stoat, digging in her bag. Suddenly—in a movement so swift that Badger nearly missed it—the stoat reached behind Badger's leg and snatched something out of the air.

"Ah!" The stoat looked at something pinched between two of her claws.

Badger felt blood drain from his face. The stoat held a tiny feather.

The stoat sniffed it. "As suspected—*Gallus gallus domesticus*." A smile curled the stoat's lips. An eyebrow rose. "Seen any chickens lately?"

Then the stoat dove.

Badger blocked the stoat with a knee.

The stoat put a foot in the door.

Badger shoved the stoat backward and said, "Stoat-gram for Badger. Now."

"Huffy, huffy, huffy. No need for that. I've got it right here." The stoat adjusted her lapel, then pulled Badger's stoat-gram out of the bag.

Badger jerked it from the stoat's grasp, pocketed it, and grabbed hold of the door.

The stoat shook her head and smiled. She held out a clipboard. "Sign."

Badger did not want to let go of the door. He narrowed his eyes at the stoat.

The stoat put her paws up. "Won't do a thing! Promise!"

Badger braced the door as best he could, took hold of the clipboard and pen, and signed. (He did not recognize his own signature.) He tossed the clipboard in the direction of the stoat, slammed the door, and drew the bolt.

Then Badger pulled the stoat-gram out of his pocket for a peek. Under "Sender" he read, "Ms. Lula P. Marten." He stuffed the stoat-gram back into the pocket, and thought, *To be read later.*

Then he drew the double bolt.

And latched the chain.

When he turned, the brownstone seemed deserted.

"Skunk? Chickens? Hello?" Badger called out.

Tiny feathers floated in the air.

"The Speedy Stoat Delivery stoat is gone!"

Skunk's head popped in. "Gone? Are you sure?"

"The stoat is gone," said Badger.

Skunk jumped into the hallway, looked both ways, and nodded. Then he stepped forward and stretched out his paw. "Who sent you a stoat-gram? Let me see!"

Badger clamped a paw over his pocket. "It is from Aunt Lula. *For me.*"

Skunk's face fell. "Aunt Lula? No! Why would she do that?"

As if it were all a great mystery, Badger laid out his paws and raised his eyebrows.

Skunk slumped. "I know why. Stoats are in the weasel family. Aunt Lula has a soft spot for *any* weasel." He straightened. "But stoats? How can she like them? She never said anything to me about stoats, or I would have shown her my bite marks!" Skunk rolled his sleeve up and pointed to a scar.

Skunk nodded. "Yes, a stoat bit me with his pointy little teeth! Quick too. Bite, bite, bite—that is a stoat! And the worst thing?" Skunk pulled over a stool, climbed on top of it, and whispered directly into Badger's ear, "Stoats drag off chickens. You never see those chickens again. We must take precautions!"

Skunk looked at Badger and waited, his eyes full of worry.

"Precautions?" Badger wasn't sure he liked the sound of that.

But now there was another sound, a squishing sound. It came from a rubber boot on his left. He looked into the boot and a chicken blinked up at him. An earflap hat on the coat stand wiggled, and out burst a bantam hen. She shook herself and floated to the floor.

"Chickens!" called Skunk. He leapt off the stool and began dashing into corners, nooks, crannies, and shadows. "You can come out now! Come out, come out!"

Like that, chickens poked their heads in. The Jersey Giant thumped down the stairs. The Ko Shamos rounded a corner. *Here today, gone to leghorn,* Badger thought, as a leghorn step-stroll-stepped into the hallway.

Skunk skidded around in greeting.

Badger searched for the tiny orange hen. He spotted her perched on the newel post at the bottom of the stairs. She had fluffed into an orange orb and was observing him with her tiny black eyes.

Meanwhile, the hallway filled with chickens: First, they covered the floorboards, then the stairs, then the tops of furniture, and then chickens landed on other chickens. (This did not go well.) Larry heaved himself into the hallway and let loose with a cough-a-doodle-hck-HCK.

Badger took that as his cue. He clapped his paws. "Time to wrap it up! Lasso that electron, hold on tight, and go wherever Quantum Leaping Chickens go at night!"

Badger felt rather clever. *Rhyming and everything!*

It was meant to be funny.

The chickens turned. They stared at Badger (left, right, left, squint-blink, squint-blink).

"The Quantum Leap does not work like that," said Skunk, his eyes flashing. "This is no time for jokes. Batten the hatches! Secure the perimeter! All bolts must be bolted! Above all else, the chickens *must* stay overnight."

"One hundred chickens overnight? Surely not!"

Skunk shot Badger a heated look.

Badger continued anyway. "My brownstone is not a chicken coop. Look, that stoat was a Speedy Stoat Delivery stoat. She is a stoat with a job to do. She is long gone by now."

Skunk marched up to him, sending chickens scrambling. "*My* brownstone? If I am your roommate, this is *our* brownstone, Badger." Skunk pointed at the door. "Do you know what happened when I opened the door? That stoat licked her eyeteeth. I am a skunk–I am not dinner!" Skunk leaned in. "Chickens are our guests!"

"Bock!" "Bock-bock!" "BOCK-bock!" said the chickens.

"Fine!" Badger exclaimed. "Do what you need to do. I am going to bed. But know this: I do not clean up after chicken sleepovers!"

Badger glanced at the newel post and saw that the tiny orange hen was no longer there.

"Bock! Bock!" said the chickens as he climbed the stairs and shut his bedroom door.

Inside his bedroom, Badger heard loud *BOCK!*-ings, the whiffling of wings, and low, troubled clucks coming from around the house.

Badger slid to the floor. *This cannot continue.*

Then he remembered: *The stoat-gram!* He patted his pocket and felt the crumple of paper. Aunt Lula had already taken care of this situation. Badger only had to read the news in Aunt Lula's stoat-gram. Badger pulled the wadded paper out of his pocket, smoothed it out, and ripped open the seal. He read:

Badger—Disappointed in you. Skunk to stay in my brownstone. If difficult after a month, contact me again.—Aunt Lula.

Badger inhaled sharply. She couldn't do this.

He looked at the paper again. She could.

Badger read the message for a third time. She *had* done it.

In a daze, Badger folded the message along its creases and got up off the floor. He walked to his desk and opened his correspondence drawer. He put the stoat-gram inside and shut it. Then he sat on the edge of his bed.

What did Aunt Lula know of dirty dishes and Laws of Nature? What did she know of boxes stamped flat and doors that banged open? Badger had seen tongs holding smoking peppers, had experienced elephants stuck in his ears. Rocket Potato still lay in Rocket Potato Corner. The kitchen oozed.

And chickens! Everywhere—chickens! "Bock-bock"? Not a language! The Quantum Leap? More tall tale than science. And now—*now!*—a one-hundred-chicken sleepover!

What about Important Rock Work? Important Rock Work must be done. *Important Rock Work!*

The whole world was against him.

Badger burrowed under the covers.

———◄◊►———

Badger stayed under the covers for fifteen minutes (give or take).

Finally, Badger declared his life, as he knew it, done. Once he had studied rocks. Once he had been an Important Rock Scientist with a diploma, three blue ribbons, and a publication file. Once he had been left alone. But all that ended here, right here, under the covers.

Badger stayed under the covers a moment longer, then he did what he needed to do. He crawled to his closet. He pulled out the ukulele, and plucked.

Pliiiinggg.

He ran his claw over the strings. *Beed . . . el . . . lee . . . bing!*

Soon a tiny tune formed.

While Skunk and the chickens latched windows and locked doors, Badger sat on the floor of his bedroom with his ukulele. The tiny tune grew.

Badger got into his pajamas and climbed into bed with his ukulele. He played the tiny tune and thought, *Maybe it isn't so bad. Let's see what tomorrow brings.*

When he had finished his tune, he put the ukulele back in its case, and slid it under his bed. He adjusted his covers, and a heaviness came upon him.

Such is the power of the ukulele, thought Badger, as he turned off the light.

With a long sigh, Badger fell asleep.

CHAPTER EIGHT

THE NEXT MORNING, VOICES ON THE BACK PORCH stirred Badger from sleep. First came a low voice. Skunk's voice followed, a short reply. Badger clutched his pillow and muttered, "Too early for social calls." Then the low voice spoke and Badger caught the cool swagger. It reminded him of someone. Someone recent. Someone not known long. He rooted sluggishly through his memory and remembered the stoat. *Irritating. Too self-assured. Yes, that's it.* Badger sighed, pulled up the covers, and began to drift off.

Skunk's voice raised in pitch. It grew higher. And louder.

The pieces dropped into place: Speedy Stoat Delivery stoat. (*Chock!*) Chickens in the brownstone. (*Chock!*) Skunk, friend of chickens. (*Chock!*)

Badger lifted an ear from the pillow and detected Skunk's tone. *Defensive—definitely defensive.* Skunk was a skunk. When skunks got defensive, they . . .

Badger sat up.

"Nooooooooooooooooooooooooooooooooooooooooooooo ooooooo!" Badger yelled as he bolted out his bedroom door, chickens scattering in every direction. "Nooooooooooooooooooo ooooooooooooooooooooooooooooooooooo!" yelled Badger as he careened down the stairs and through the hallway to the back door.

He tossed the door open. Badger saw Skunk with teeth bared, lips folded back, and tail upright! "Nooooooooooooooooooooooo oooooooooooooooooooooooooooo!"

Later, Badger would reflect that flying *toward* Skunk had not been the best strategy, particularly when he'd glimpsed the back end of the stoat sprinting off in the opposite direction—*away.* Also, how had he missed the hiss of vaporization?

But never mind. Yelling "Nooooooooooo!" Badger pushed off, limbs outstretched, flying *toward* Skunk. Time slowed. The flight seemed to go on forever. Badger saw Skunk notice him and step aside. Then Badger hit the spray, and though he was no stranger to the smell of skunk, Badger had never before showered in it.

Noooooooooooooooooooooooooooooooooooooooo!

And this was a shower, a showering in an oily stink, a stink that stuck. It glazed his snout, his furry face, the fine hairs of his eyebrows. Badger balled up.

And dropped.

And skidded to a stop. Full stop.

Badger lay on the porch, coughing, gasping for one gulp of clean, clear air. (It was not forthcoming.) His eyes watered. His snout quivered and ran. Badger wiped at them with his furry forearm, but to no avail. Everything watered. *I am a spigot!* he thought, as he pressed his forearm to his snout and scraped himself into a seated position.

Next to him, Skunk leaned over, his paws on his knees, breathing heavily. Then Skunk straightened up and stretched. He rolled his neck one way, the other.

Snout to forearm, Badger gawked. Skunk exhibited no ill effects. *Not one!* Skunk combed through his stripe with two claws as he gazed across the backyard to the alley beyond. He shook out his limbs, turned to Badger, and whispered, "I would not like to meet that stoat again." Then a smile spread across his face. "Did you see that atomization, Badger? Impressive. Bye-bye stoat! Ha!" Skunk closed his eyes and danced, pumping his paws into the air.

"Hck! Hck! HCCccK!" Badger coughed into his forearm.

"ALL CLEAR, CHICKENS. THE STOAT IS GONE. THE STOAT TURNED AND RAN. Yes, she did, yes she did!"

Badger looked up and saw Skunk at the back door.

From the kitchen came a sound remarkably similar to the sound of a standing ovation. Badger knew it was only the clapping of wings as one hundred chickens gathered. Still, Badger winced. He wiped his nose in fury on his now-sodden forearm.

Skunk shut the door. He met Badger's gaze with a wide smile and shrugged. "There is always, ah, a lingering aroma, but look at how well it works! Everything is a-okay now, Badger." Skunk dusted off his paws. "I am going to need a long nap."

A-okay? Lingering aroma? Time for a nap? The stink hung in the air, blossoming in every direction. It was rotten eggs, old coffee, and mushroomy, stuck-to-the-bottom garbage goo. It burned like chili peppers. It puckered like lemons. Badger was steeped in it, had flown through it, and now carried it.

"You have some explaining to do," Badger growled.

Skunk flinched. He looked at Badger in surprise. "I will see to the chickens," he said quickly. In he went. The door slammed shut.

Badger was alone.

Badger sat in a funk and stewed. Finally, he pulled himself up off the porch floorboards and followed Skunk into the brownstone. He clutched at the first available dish towel and blew his snout into it. "Pffft–TOOOOOTpfffff, pfft . . . pfft." Then he mopped himself up, pressed the towel over his snout, and noticed the silence in the kitchen. He looked up.

The kitchen did not easily accommodate one hundred chickens. The birds had bunched. One deluge of chickens and behold, feathered life! Badger saw not a kitchen, but a chicken biome of the Tropical Chicken Forest sort. Every surface burst forth in feathers. Cabinetry quilled. Right angles went soft and blowy. But this wasn't plant–this was animal. Now the chicken biome observed Badger with each of its two hundred eyes (right-left-right, blink, blink).

A sound caught his attention.

Drip. Drip. Drip.

Badger followed the sound and saw Skunk standing at the counter, holding a ladle. A bowl of batter and a square gadget rested on the counter next to him. The gadget's red light blinked. A glop of something batterish dropped from the ladle.

Drip.

Eyes on Skunk, Badger stepped to the counter.

Skunk looked over his shoulder and gave a start. "Oh. Badger. There you are. Right there. Good morning. No, not *good*. But it is morning. That is true." Batter spooled to the counter. *DrrripP.* "Would you like a waffle? We are eating waffles." Skunk flashed Badger a tiny smile.

A trio of speckled hens stepped out of the understory. Badger saw a plate of waffles on the floor. One of the hens kicked a waffle in Badger's direction. The waffle skittered off the plate.

"Bock?" The hen eyed him (right, left, right).

Skunk hurriedly retrieved the waffle. "I will make you a fresh waffle. The chickens have been picking at their waffles this morning, which is understandable given the circumstances."

Understandable? Badger huffed into his dish towel and noticed the air was filled with under-feathers. There'd been a chicken sleepover. Now chickens, and chicken whatsits, covered his kitchen. Batter was dripping! Then Badger got a whiff of himself and nearly passed out.

Mid-swoon, Badger looked into the corner and saw it. *Rocket Potato!*

"You owe me an apology," Badger snarled.

Skunk shook his head. "Apologize? Why? Badger, I do not think I was the problem." He gestured toward the porch.

"That Speedy Stoat Delivery stoat was in our back garden this morning. I told that stoat she was most unwelcome. I told her that delivering and leaving was her job. But she would not go away, and she had been there all night! Then she came to her pointy-toothed point: She says she will leave if I give her a chicken. Give her a chicken? *Give* her? Chickens are their own chickens. No one *gives* a chicken!"

"Bock!" "Bock-bock!" exclaimed four bantam hens stalking the floor.

"You're welcome," Skunk whispered.

Badger waved his paws (and the damp dish towel with them). "No, this will not do. You have soiled my place of work, defiled it, mucked it all up. You sprayed in my brownstone!"

Skunk frowned up at Badger. "Technically, it is Aunt Lula's brownstone. And I did not spray *in* the brownstone. I sprayed on the back porch—where there is a brisk breeze!"

"You *sprayed*. Everyone knows that skunk spray is despicable, deplorable, vile. You could have woken me up. Why didn't you wake me up? I am not afraid of a tiny stoat!" Badger glowered down at Skunk.

Skunk's tail began twitching back and forth like a whip. He took a step toward Badger. "Okay, let me tell you how it was. This morning I told myself, 'Skunk, Badger is right. You have filled up on fears. A Speedy Stoat Delivery stoat is a stoat with a job to do. That stoat will not be in the back garden.' But I could not let the chickens go home until I had made sure the stoat was gone, so I went outside, by myself, to take a look. By myself! And Badger? It is too late to wake up badgers when you are standing in front of a stoat!"

Badger felt crowded by feathery poofs, beaks, and peering eyes (right, left, right).

Skunk continued, his eyes on fire: "Then Ms. Pointy-tooth moved toward me. I told that stoat to stop. I gave her a good look at my tail. Believe me, she knew what was coming! And–for the record–spraying is not so bad when you consider that I left that stoat smelly but unharmed. That stoat would not have been so nice to me. I would be lucky to get away at all! So yes, the brownstone smells, and yes, you smell, Badger. But our guests are safe. I am safe. And that stoat is now a smarter stoat. I am sorry for the smell, Badger, but it will pass."

A "grrrrr" rumbled through Badger's throat as he realized this was his apology.

But no one listened. The chickens broke into squawks. They flapped up off the floor, raising a cloud of chicken dander. It all sounded suspiciously like a second round of applause.

"You sprayed me," Badger said.

"That was not my fault. You leapt!" Skunk replied.

Badger ground his teeth, put the dish towel to his dribbling eyes, and muttered, "And they wonder why no one wants to live with them! Skunks are the true nuisance animal."

The kitchen went quiet.

Skunk let out a *huh*. When he spoke it was with a weak voice. "Did you call me a *nuisance animal*?"

Badger fidgeted.

But what about his apology?

Badger said nothing. He spotted the little orange hen. She appeared to be avoiding Badger's gaze.

Skunk squinted at Badger and blinked as if the sight scalded. Then Skunk began to do some sort of math on his claws. "Despicable, deplorable, vile," he mumbled and put out three claws. "Spoiling, defiling." He put out another two claws. "Nuisance animal," he said. Now six claws on two paws were out. "Skunks lumped together in a generality. Also, other insults." Skunk stared at his paws. "Eight claws," he mumbled. His shoulders drooped.

Skunk looked up at Badger and nodded. "You think I'm vermin. You think the world would be better off without skunks."

Badger shook his head. "I did not say that!"

"You did. I added it up: nuisance, defiling, spoiling, despicable, deplorable, vile, and you said *skunks*, with an *s*. General insults

. . . eeeeeeeeeeeeeeeeeeeeeeeeeee . . .

. . . *eeeeeeeeeeeee . . . eeeeeeee . . . eee . . .*

too. That adds up to the definition of vermin," said Skunk. He nodded his head vigorously.

"I would *not* say that!"

But Skunk no longer appeared to hear him.

"There is only one thing to be done," Skunk said as he left the room.

"BOCK?" said the Jersey Giant.

Skunk's "one thing" did not take long. In a blow of the snout and a wipe of the eyes on the dish towel, it was done. Skunk stood in the kitchen. In one paw was the small red suitcase tied shut with twine. With the other, he gave Badger his key.

Badger took it.

Skunk shook Badger's paw. "It was nice to meet you. I had heard so much about you from Aunt Lula."

Without thinking, Badger said the polite thing to say: "Maybe we'll meet another time?"

Skunk shook his head and looked away. "I doubt it. Animals that do not like skunks *really* do not like skunks. Not everyone wants a skunk."

"Oh. Goodbye?" said Badger.

Skunk hung his head. "Bye."

The chickens left with Skunk. Badger watched from the porch (blowing his snout, blotting his eyes). There at the front was Skunk, a small, black-and-white animal holding a red suitcase tied up with twine. Behind him followed the chickens, filling the alleyway with tufts and red wattles, yellow legs and flaps of wings.

Badger thought, *Isn't this what you wanted?*

CHAPTER NINE

BADGER WAS ALONE IN THE BROWNSTONE. TINY FEATHERS eddied back and forth in the air. The brownstone stank. He stank.

Badger rushed up the stairs to the bathroom and scrubbed his entire head.

Toweling off, Badger noticed he was still wearing his pajamas. He would have liked a bath and a change of outfit, but now that his head had been soaped, he didn't seem to mind his own smell as much. *First things first.* Badger went up to his bedroom to write a letter.

Badger sat down at his desk, took out a piece of stationery, and wrote, "Dear Aunt Lula."

He tapped his pencil. *Aunt Lula must be informed—Skunk sprayed!* he told himself. *In addition, I must mention that I had nothing to do with Skunk moving out.*

"You think I'm a vermin," Badger heard Skunk say in his head.

"But I didn't say that word!" Badger said out loud. Furiously, Badger scribbled, "Dear Aunt Lula."

He saw he'd already written this. "Sludge and slurry!"

Badger dropped his pencil, crumpled the stationery, and thunked open his dictionary. He flipped to the letter *v*, and ran his claw down a page. He stopped at "vermin" and hunched over to read.

Badger read. He thought.

He read the definition again. And thought again.

Then Badger slowly closed the dictionary. He let out a long, low sigh.

I must speak to Skunk! Now! Badger stood up and grabbed his brownstone key. On the way out the door, he pulled on his coat.

Badger stopped on the stoop of the brownstone. He looked to the left, the direction Skunk and the chickens had gone. But up that way was only Queggly Hill Park. *A park? Unlikely!* This was hardly an occasion for amusement and leisure.

Badger looked to the right. The town of North Twist sprawled in every direction. When had North Twist gotten so big? Had there always been so many shops? Was that a hotel? Badger had not noticed the Double-Dice Game Shop, or the shop with a sign that read Books, or the Hot Pie Now sign.

HOT PIE NOW? Badger did a double take. Sure enough, there was a pie sign flashing in the window of the Veg & Egger Diner. How had he missed pie?

At least I recognize Posey the Toad's Grocery Store, Badger thought. Yes, he knew Posey's! Every Tuesday Badger visited the grocery store, pushing his cart up and down the same three aisles and filling it with the same fourteen items. At the register, Badger said "Good day" to Posey and paid with exact change. Posey replied, saying whatever she said, and Badger ignored her, his mind on Important Rock Work. *Focus, focus, focus*, he always told himself as he walked the sidewalk back to the brownstone.

But now, Badger shook his head and thought, *It is problematic that I do not know North Twist. How will I know where to start looking?* Badger recalled what he knew of Skunk: Skunk had a red suitcase tied up with twine. Inside the suitcase were pajamas, a storybook, and a chicken whistle. Skunk liked to cook. Skunk liked chickens.

It is problematic that I do not know North Twist.

Chickens! A chicken would know where to find Skunk.

Badger looked. There were no chickens in that direction or that direction. Or that direction.

Then Badger noticed something written in cursive above the Books on the bookstore's sign. Badger took another look. "Har! Har!" The sign above the store read CHICKEN BOOKS!

With a spring, Badger stepped off the stoop of the brownstone.

———◄○►———

Chicken Books had *two* doorknobs, one at chicken height. Badger took hold of the higher doorknob.

"Cock-a-doodle-BING," sounded the door as he pushed it open.

"Oh," said Badger, as he stepped inside. Chicken Books felt like a book terrarium. Books were lined up on long, sunlit tables. Books wound around the walls. Badger longed to stretch his limbs, sip the warm air, and settle in a chair with a book from the Rock Books section. (*Rock Books!*)

But now was not the time for leisurely reading. Badger scanned the bookstore. A pig and a hare leaned over a book. Two crows perched on top of a display. Underneath a table, a field mouse read a book in a section labeled: FOR OUR SMALLEST READERS: LEAST BUT NEVER LAST.

No chickens, he thought.

Badger made a circuit through the store. A carrier pigeon perched in the Chicken Little the Mighty section. In the Chick Lit section, a sign read: BOARD BOOKS GUARANTEED TO WITHSTAND *ANY* CHICK! But there were no chicks in Chick Lit, only two piglets roughhousing. Badger found it odd that no one said hello or stopped to ask if they could help him find a book. Where were the store clerks? Additionally, all the customers read with concentration.

Badger ended up at the checkout counter. *No chickens here either.*

A sign above the old-fashioned cash register read, BOOKS BOUGHT AND QUESTIONS ANSWERED HERE. The arrow underneath the word HERE pointed at a smaller sign. Badger hunched to read it. It read, WRITE YOUR QUESTIONS DOWN. BUY YOUR BOOKS LATER. A nubby pencil lay next to the sign, along with a heap of scrap paper.

On the other side of the cash register was a stack of business cards. Badger picked one up and read, "Chicken Books is chicken-owned and operated. (Bookstore run as hens see fit.)" He looked around. *Where are the chickens?*

Badger heard a rustle of newspaper. He turned and saw a hedgehog wearing a tam o'shanter peeking out from behind the *New Yak Times Book Review*. Their eyes met. The hedgehog shook his paper, tilted his head meaningfully toward his reading, and disappeared behind the *Book Review*.

Badger tapped the *Book Review*. "Excuse me. Do you know where I could find a store clerk or a chicken?"

The hedgehog lowered the newspaper. "You're Badger, correct? The badger that lives in Lula P. Marten's brownstone?"

"Yes," said Badger, surprised.

"I believe the chickens think you would give them to a stoat," the hedgehog said, pushing up an edge of his tam o'shanter and adjusting his reading glasses.

"What did you say?" said Badger, blinking.

"Surely, you know what I mean," said the hedgehog. "We've all heard. *And* smelled! Also, your own odor has taken on an irrefutable skunkiness. This leads to my conclusion that you must be *that* badger, Badger." The hedgehog turned a page of the *New Yak Times Book Review*.

"Oh . . . Oh . . . I see." Badger glanced around the bookstore in horror. The hare looked away, examined her paws, and picked up a paperback. The pig's snout was mashed into the spine of an open hardcover. And when Badger turned back to the hedgehog in the tam o'shanter, he found the hedgehog gone. the *Book Review* lay in a crumple on the floor, smudged with small paw prints.

Badger thought of the tiny orange hen and winced.

He opened his mouth. He looked one way, then the other, and . . . fled.

"Cock-a-doodle-BING."

———◁◦▷———

So they knew. Everyone knew.

Badger spied a bench around the corner from Chicken Books and raced for it. He slid into a seated position, and tucked his head between his knees. That's when he noticed that he'd left the brownstone wearing his pajamas—his particularly vibrant pickaxe-and-dynamite pajamas.

"No, no, no." Pajamas in public only happened in nightmares!

Badger began listing recent events in his mind: The chickens thought Badger would give them to a stoat. Badger had said those awful things that added up to "vermin" to Skunk. And there was this: Aunt Lula had sent the stoat-gram *in response* to Badger's letter. So who had started all of this? Badger, Badger, Badger.

It was a nightmare, the worst kind—a nightmare of his own making.

Badger thought of the tiny orange hen. He thought of the leghorn, the Orpingtons, the Orloff, the Transylvania Naked Necks. *Larry!* Badger pictured Skunk, his red suitcase tied up with twine in one paw. "Not everyone wants a skunk," Skunk had said.

Badger put his head in his paws. His heart ached.

———◦———

Several minutes later, Badger wiped his eyes and stood. He would say he was sorry. He would see if he could make amends. But first, he needed to find Skunk. Or the chickens. Or both Skunk *and* the chickens.

Across the street was a hotel. Maybe Skunk had booked a room.

It was a good idea, but Badger did not cross the street. He stood on the curb and stared at the hotel. He felt a strong urge to run back to the brownstone and never, ever, *ever* come out.

Finally Badger thought, *If everyone knows what I have done, there is nothing to hide.*

But he was wearing pickaxe-and-dynamite pajamas.

At least they're nonrestrictive—sweat-wicking too, he told himself.

His pajamas reeked.

Surely I am not the first animal with stinky pajamas!

And with that, Badger stepped off the sidewalk and crossed the street.

———◦———

The vole at the hotel's front reception desk said Skunk had been there. Skunk had told her all about a rabbit who sucked a magician into his top hat using a shop vac: "*Vvvvoooooooop̄P̄!*–no more magician!" But Skunk had not checked into the Twisty Hotel.

"Hey, do you know that the chickens think you'd give them to a stoat?" said the vole as Badger left.

Hastily, Badger shut the door.

————◄o►————

"Oh yeah–the shoehorn skunk!" said the salamander at the Double-Dice Game Shop. He slapped a rubbery knee. "Said he wanted shoehorns and marched all around, elbows out, making horn-bleats with every step. Then he says, 'Or are those only available from door-to-door sales animals?' I had to tell him what shoehorns are. His face hit the rug. Hit. The. Rug. He says, '*Shoehorn* is the most disappointing word I have ever heard!' I had to agree with him."

The salamander had not seen Skunk that morning.

As Badger made to leave, the salamander grabbed Badger's forearm. "Have you heard what the chickens think?" he said.

"Yes, I know what the chickens think!" said Badger, shaking himself free.

"Have a good day!" called the salamander as Badger bolted through the door.

———◄○►———

Badger searched for Skunk and the chickens all morning long. He walked up and down sidewalks. He went in and out of shops. He spoke to shop clerks. He stopped shoppers. The animals that spoke to him made observations (that he stank, that he wore pajamas). They told him what they thought of his behavior (bad), and tacked on advice. How to apologize was a popular topic: "You must hear yourself say 'I am sorry' out loud," said a woodchuck. A brown bat added, "Don't say 'I'm sorry *but* this' or 'I'm sorry *but* that.'" "Make sure to listen," whispered a box turtle. All of them asked if he knew what the chickens thought. He did! He did! Sigh—yes. And for good reason!

In the end though—after all that—Badger was no closer to finding Skunk or a single chicken.

———◄○►———

Finally, it was two o'clock and Badger found himself staring at the neon HOT PIE NOW sign at the Veg & Egger. He suspected his motives for staring were not purely informational.

And then, he noticed the diner's name, and thought, *Veg &*
Egger . . . Egger . . . Egg. Yes, egg . . .

He spoke what came to him: "Q-U-*egg*-L-Y." Queggly Hill
Park!

It's worth a try, thought Badger.

He got a quick hot paw-pie from the Veg & Egger—*Hey, was*
that waitress a female badger?—and was on his way.

But before Badger headed up the hill, he needed to stop at
the brownstone to make preparations.

CHAPTER TEN

BACK AT THE BROWNSTONE, BADGER UNLOCKED THE front door and was greeted by the stuffy fug of skunk spray. "Sludge and slurry!" He waved his paws and held his breath. He would do what he needed to do and do it fast.

In the kitchen, he made a chicken gift and scooped it into a paper sack. Then he jogged to the coat closet where he kept his rock expedition knapsack at the ready. The knapsack contained a hard hat, protective goggles, a tool belt, a utility knife, a chisel, a hammer, specimen bags, a flashlight, a hand lens on a lanyard, a pencil magnet, a compass, two snack bars, a full water bottle, and one waterproof ukulele. Badger tucked his chicken gift into the top of the pack, swung the pack onto his back, and left the brownstone.

As Badger headed up the hill, he ate his paw-pie from the Veg & Egger. *Delicious!* Badger thought, licking cinnamon apple goo from between his claws. He whistled as he followed the sidewalk. *I must get out more. More walks! More pie!*

Thirty minutes later, Badger stopped at the top of the hill. The arch in front of him read: QUEGGLY HILL PARK. He examined the spelling. *Egg—definitely egg.* Then he stepped underneath the arch and into the park.

———◇———

Badger liked Queggly Hill Park right away. *Why haven't I been up here?* he wondered. Queggly Hill Park had everything necessary for a good day. Badger took inventory: one picnic table, one swing set with three swings (*Suitable for competitions!*), one seesaw, one slide, and one paw-pump for pumping water. It had the right trees too: over here, thick-limbed climbing trees; over there, smooth-trunked reading trees with lots of shade. And a boulder! Badger always preferred a park with boulders. He patted the boulder, felt its coolness, and nodded appreciatively. *Granite.*

But there was a problem. *No chickens.*

Badger looked around. Worse than no chickens—Queggly Hill Park was utterly deserted. He couldn't even ask anyone if they'd *seen* a chicken. Where was everyone?

"Hello? Chickens? Hello? I'm here to say I'm sorry," Badger called out.

A tickle of wind circled Badger's ankles.

"Hello? Anyone?"

No birdsong. No chiding squirrels. Not even the sound of anyone kicking up a snack in the leaf litter!

Badger turned slowly in a full circle and realized that he'd now seen the entirety of Queggly Hill Park. It had taken all of, say, three minutes. Queggly Hill Park was officially minuscule.

But Badger wasn't ready to give up. *I have found rocks. I will find chickens.* He tugged off his rock expedition knapsack, set it on the picnic table, and unzipped it. He put on his tool belt, the protective goggles, and his hard hat, and got to work.

Badger examined. He scraped and sifted. He sniffed and tasted (tentatively). Light beamed from his flashlight. He poked around leaves, turned over stones, and spoke to pill bugs. (The pill bugs curled.) He appraised bluebells, trillium, and bloodroot through his hand lens. All spiderwebs were scrutinized.

Finally, Badger removed his hard hat and protective goggles and shook out his specimen bag onto the picnic table.

Two twigs and five dirt clumps.

"That's it?" he said in disgust. But there'd been no signs of chickens: no chicken dander, no chicken fluff, no whistles, no sheboxes, no storybooks, and no paper receipts from Chicken Books. Badger was about to swipe the entire mess off the boulder when he saw something poking out of a dirt clod. It looked fluff-ish.

He broke the clod apart, pinched it up, and examined it. The fluff glimmered in a way that seemed partial to the color orange.

Could it be? Badger reached for his hand lens . . .

. . . and a puff of wind blew the fluff away.

"No!" yelled Badger, thumping his fist on the picnic table.

He sat down on the picnic bench. He ran a paw through his stripe. *Think, think, think,* he said to himself.

But to no avail—Badger had run out of ideas. It was over. Badger stood up and slowly packed his rock-finding gear into his knapsack. As he packed, his paw brushed the paper sack.

Badger pulled out the paper sack and stared at it. *What do I have to lose?*

Not one thing, Badger decided. He pulled on his knapsack and got started. He reached inside the sack, filled his paw, and tossed.

Popcorn flew.

"Here chickie-chickie. Here chickie-chickie-chickie," he called.

He reached into the paper sack again, and tossed another paw-full of popcorn. "Here chickie!"

He glanced around. No chickens. Not one.

Badger spoke louder: "Here chickie, chickie, chickie," and tossed another paw-full of popcorn into the air.

He looked. No chickens.

"Chickie? Chickie? CHICKEEE-EE!" He tossed popcorn left and right, right and left. He began to skip. He skipped around the slide and tossed his popcorn. "Chickie, chickie, HERE!" He put his belly on the swing seat and swung, to-ing and fro-ing as he threw. "POPCORN CHICKIE!" He leapt onto the picnic table. "COME CHICKIE!" He surfed the seesaw and threw another paw-full up, up, UP. "CHICKIE-CHICK POPCORN!" He bounced. He vaulted. He twirled. He tossed. He tripped and tossed and skipped off again.

Then the bag was empty. *Shake, shake? Shake?*

An unpopped kernel hit his right foot.

Still no chickens.

Zip. Zzzttt.

What had *he been thinking? Just because there is an "egg" cracked into the middle of "Queggly" does not mean there will be chickens.*

Badger walked to the boulder. He dropped to his knees and tore off his knapsack. He flopped onto his back, and lay splayed on the boulder like the letter *X*.

—◄◦►—

After quite some time, Badger sat up. He rubbed his knees, and then his shoulder, and thought, *Skunk was right—rocks are hard.*

Then Badger saw the view. It looked like an illustration, sketched out in pencil and colored in bright greens. There was North Twist wrapped in hills, knotted with trees, and laced with sidewalks and walking paths. A stream meandered through a field on Badger's left. To Badger's right were brownstones, then bungalows, then wildly painted Victorians with rocking-chair porches.

Badger wondered what Skunk would say if he were here.

"Har!" Badger knew exactly what Skunk would say. Skunk would point and say, *Look, Badger, that is where you were.*

So Badger looked as he thought Skunk would look. He found Aunt Lula's brownstone. He spotted the meadow across the street. He traced part of his route—Chicken Books to the Twisty Hotel to the Double-Dice Game Shop.

The HOT PIE NOW sign was still on. Badger thought, *I should take Skunk out for some paw-pie!*

Then Badger realized this was never, *ever* going to happen. He was not even going to get to apologize—not today anyway.

The sun was setting.

He had failed.

Badger wiped his eyes and blew his snout. He had behaved badly. He'd said things. He'd *done* things. He'd *not* done things.

His behavior had revealed things about him that he'd rather not know and now he knew. He should change. But he was a badger set in his ways. It would be just like him to fall right back into his old patterns and not make a single change.

Still, I must try.

He stared at the view of North Twist for a long moment. Then he tugged his rock expedition knapsack to him and took out his waterproof ukulele. He tucked the ukulele under his left elbow, lifted his right paw, and strummed. *Beed-el-lee-bing!*

He strummed again. *Beed-el-lee-bing!*

And then, the power of the ukulele took hold. Badger's claws began to ricochet over the strings. The ukulele rattled. Badger sang, then bellowed:

> *E huli, e huli mākou*
> *E huli, e huli mākou*
> *Kou maka, kou lima,*
> *Me kou kino eeeeeeeeeeeeeeeeeeeeeeeeeeeeeeeeeeeeeeeeeeeeeee* . . .

It was the C7 chord, the chord heading into the song's resolve. But Badger did not want to resolve, to finish, to move on. So Badger kept singing the *eeeeeeeeeeeeeeeee*, holding on to the note and beating out the C7 chord.

113

". . . eeeeeeeeeeeeeeeeeeeeeeeeeee . . ."

The sky had gone red with twists of apricot, pumpkin, carrot, and coral. North Twist shimmered in gold.

". . . eeeeeeeeeeeeee . . . eeeeeeeee . . . eee . . ."

The air drained from Badger's lungs, but still his claws banged over the strings: C7, C7, C7, and still he sang:

". . . eeeeeeeeeeeeeee . . . eee . . . eeeeeeeee . . . eeee . . ."

Badger saw one star, then two stars.

". . . ee . . . ee . . . e . . . eeee . . . eee . . ."

C7 . . . C7 . . . C7 . . .

"*E aloha mai!* G7! C7! F!" came a yell from behind him.

CHAPTER ELEVEN

"THE UKULELE IS THE MOST BEAUTIFUL INSTRUMENT IN the world!"

Badger knew that voice. He jumped to his feet.

"Skunk?"

Skunk saw him and backed up. "Oh no," he said, turning and starting the other way.

"Wait! I've looked everywhere for you," Badger called.

Skunk's back stiffened. Slowly, he twisted back around. He fidgeted, but stood. He stood at a good distance.

In order to make sure Skunk heard, Badger yelled. "I AM SORRY FOR THE WAY I BEHAVED. EVEN THOUGH I DIDN'T SAY 'VERMIN,' I CALLED YOU THE DEFINITION OF VERMIN. I AM SORRY FOR THAT.

ALSO, YOU DEFENDED OUR GUESTS. I DID NOTHING. I DID NOT EVEN LISTEN TO YOU. I AM SORRY FOR THAT TOO. AND I HAVE NOT WELCOMED YOU INTO THE BROWNSTONE. YOU HAVE AS MUCH RIGHT TO THE BROWNSTONE AS I DO."

Badger swallowed. What he yelled next was something he'd decided as he lay flat on the boulder: "THE BROWNSTONE IS YOURS. I'M MOVING OUT."

Skunk's head jerked back with a shake.

Skunk walked closer. "Would you say that again please, but in a quieter voice?"

"I'm letting you have the brownstone. I'm moving out."

Skunk marched right up under Badger's snout. "But the brownstone is your home!"

"And now it's yours," said Badger, nodding. He felt lighter. "Har! Har!"

Skunk shook his head. "This is not funny, Badger. You own too many rocks. You cannot carry all of them in a suitcase."

"Simplicity is good," said Badger. "I will cut down!"

Skunk held up a paw to think. Finally, with hesitation, he nodded. "Simplicity has its advantages. Yes, it *is* nice when everything fits in a red suitcase, but it is *nicer* to have a Moon

Room and a good kitchen. Believe me, being without a home is not good."

He squinted up at Badger. "What about your Important Rock Work?"

Badger blurted the first thing that came to mind. "I will focus on fieldwork. I'll live in a tent and travel. I'll discover new rocks."

"Oh," said Skunk. He looked surprised. "I see." He appeared to be thinking, but Badger could not read his thoughts.

Badger waited.

Finally, Skunk laughed. "Ha! Are you wearing pajamas? Yes, you are. Those are the same pajamas you were wearing this morning!"

Badger looked down. "I've been wearing them all over North Twist."

They laughed together, and then Skunk sighed. He looked up at Badger. "Okay, I will move back into the brownstone. I like chickens a lot, but Badger, skunks are not meant to live in henhouses. Still . . ." He shook his head and kicked at a loose rock.

Badger stared in disbelief. "You should be happy. The brownstone is yours."

Skunk shot Badger a look. "Not everyone is like you, Badger! I do not like living alone. Now I will have to look for a roommate. Yes, the brownstone is better than a henhouse, but all alone? The brownstone is big for one skunk."

"I'll be your roommate!" Badger blurted out.

Then he realized what he had said. "Forget it! Unless you want me as a roommate. Which I would like . . ."

That didn't make sense. Or did it? So Badger added, "I said that because I've missed you. Nothing has been the same since you left."

Skunk frowned at Badger. "I have only been gone since this morning."

"I know. But I have missed you," Badger mumbled.

Skunk's eyes grew round.

Then Skunk nodded. "Okay."

"Okay what?" said Badger.

"Okay, you can be my roommate. But first we need to discuss things."

"What things?" said Badger, alarmed.

Skunk leaned forward, looked both ways, and whispered, "The chickens like the rock room too much. Would it be possible to move your rock room out of the living room? Anyway, the living room would be better as a living room—with comfy chairs, board games, and lots of books."

Badger sighed. "What about the attic?"

"Perfect. But that rock shaker . . ." said Skunk.

"Rock *tumbler*. I'm a rock scientist—I like my rock tumbler!"

"Okay. Moon Room?"

"Is exactly as you left it. It is yours."

"If I cook?"

"I clean. Law of Nature."

"Deal. Roommates!" Skunk stuck out a paw. They shook on it, both of them grinning ear to ear.

Then Skunk pointed. "Look."

Badger turned. There, on the boulder, a tiny orange poof. The tiny orange hen! She observed the two of them (left eye, right eye, left eye).

"Bock?"

Badger put his head near hers. "I am sorry."

The little orange hen pecked his snout. Then she did it again.

"Ow." Badger sat up. "I deserved that. I did."

"She has been upset," said Skunk with a chuckle. Then he asked, "Badger, may I play your ukulele?"

Keeping his eyes on the hen, Badger passed back his ukulele.

Beed-el-lee-bing! sounded the ukulele, as the little orange hen hopped onto Badger's knee.

"Bock," she said.

"I mean it. I'm sorry." Badger picked some of the popcorn off the boulder, and put it in the palm of his paw.

Beed-el-lee-bing!

The hen looked at him (right-left-right, blink). Then she hopped onto his paw and chose a piece of popcorn, and Badger understood that he was forgiven.

When Badger lifted his eyes, he saw that chickens filled Queggly Hill Park. There were Orpingtons, Naked Necks, and Dominickers. The Orloff strutted by. The Jersey Giant plonked her feet down on the grass. Tiny bantam hens bantered with long-legged striders. There were many breeds of chickens that Badger had never seen before.

All the chickens ate popcorn. A few brought out their shoeboxes.

Badger looked at Skunk. "How do the chickens suddenly appear like that?"

Skunk smiled. "The Quantum Leap? I told you, chickens are wondrous."

"Har! Yes, they are!" Then Badger pointed at a chicken who zigged, then zagged, and disappeared behind the seesaw. "Here today, gone to leghorn," he said.

Skunk laughed. "Ha! That is what I always say."

Skunk sat next to Badger and the orange hen. Together the three of them watched as the sky deepened into reds and purples, all of it eventually dissolving into evening blue.

Beed-el-lee-bing!

"This is better than fireworks," said Skunk.

Badger looked at Skunk and nodded. "I am so glad we are going to be roommates, Skunk."

"Me too. What a relief!"

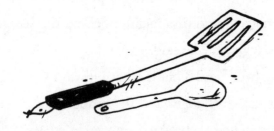

THE BEGINNING

IT WAS BREAKFAST—SOMETIME THE NEXT WEEK—WHEN IT happened: Skunk set a plate of fried egg, potatoes, and parsnips in front of Badger, and then Skunk stopped.

"Rocket Potato!" he yelled.

Skunk hop-skipped to the corner. Ever so gently, he plucked up the potato and brushed it off.

"Look, Badger." Skunk held out his cupped paws.

Badger saw a greenish, wrinkled potato.

Skunk pointed at two white horns. "Rocket Potato wants to live," he whispered.

"Why, look at that," said Badger.

Skunk nodded. "Let's plant it and see what it makes of itself."

So that's what they did.

ACKNOWLEDGMENTS

A FEW PEOPLE AND SOURCES NEED MENTIONING: IN 1997, Jerry W. Dragoo and Rodney L. Honeycutt kicked skunks out of the weasel family, elevating skunks to the level of family thereafter known as the Mephitidae. This explains much family drama. (Find "Systematics of Mustelid-like Carnivores" in the *Journal of Mammalogy* 78[2]: 426-443, 1997.) Natalie Angier made the chickens' world a safer place. If I had not listened to the audiobook of *The Canon: A Whirligig Tour of the Beautiful Basics of Science*, the chickens would not have "the Quantum Leap!" (I always hear this said in Skunk's voice.) Though I used several sources for the geology, Jim Miller is the geologist who put twenty of us in traffic safety vests so we could stand beside a busy highway and squint up at road cuts. That said, all mistakes (and simplifications) in this book are my own. I'm also grateful to the North House Folk School in Grand Marais, Minnesota, for offering a geology course for enthusiastic beginners. Lanialoha Lee introduced me to the wonders of the ukulele and taught me the song "E Huli Mākou." My agent, Steven Malk, worked patiently and persistently to find a home for this story. The book you are holding would not exist without him. I'm indebted to my editor, Elise Howard, at Algonquin Young Readers, for taking on and editing this project, and to Jon Klassen, who agreed early to provide his beautiful art. Phil, my husband, reads my work first. This project has been a joy for both of us. Thank you for that, Phil!